# WEDDING DAY

## THE GATES OF INLAND
### BOOK SIX

## JOHN ROSEGRANT

MITHRIL HOUSE

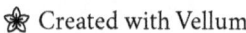

*For Donna and Joey*

# CONTENTS

# RATTLED

*I*t would be hard enough to lose a giant woman, but a giant lion too?

As a threesome they had stepped into the gateway, the woman holding Dan's left hand, the lion's mane wrapped in his right. But no matter how many times Dan shook and clenched his hands, both were empty now.

The gate blinked out behind him. If the woman and lion had held back in the Shadowlands, it was all over. The Shadowlands were tricky and shifting and Dan could never find them there again, especially without his magical girlfriend Maggie. Worse yet, he had lost Maggie too and he needed the woman and lion to help him rescue her. Dan kicked the ground so hard that he stubbed his toe through his hard boot. But that drew his eye to a mark in the dirt, and he knelt to see better.

A normal-size paw print he might not have spotted in the pale moonlight, but this was huge. They had come through with him! They were somewhere in Outland—the normal world.

But that created another problem: Dan had intentionally

brought them to this exact spot in Outland, the Goth Woods behind his old high school, because there shouldn't be anybody here to see them this time of night. But if they wandered into town there was going to be a huge uproar. He could just imagine explaining it to the cops:

"You see, Officer, this is First Changing Beast. What? Yes, I know that we have here a woman as well as a beast, but that's because of the 'changing' part. It takes other forms too: Sometimes it looks like just one creature, a lion with a human body, and sometimes it's just a woman who is bulkier than this one. Maybe it has other forms I haven't even seen, but I don't want to think about that. Why does she have hardly any clothes on? Well, you see, that outfit is just right for where I found her, prehistoric Africa. What's that? Yes, prehistoric Africa, maybe a million years ago. I know it sounds crazy, but this is about the magical world of Inland. You see, I was summoned to Inland and given a quest to rescue First Changing Beast. Inland is the world our fairy tales come from, and it used to be connected with our world by gates, but the gates have been closing and they need to get First Changing Beast back to keep them open.

"Stop! Please put those handcuffs away and listen to me. It turns out First Changing Beast was being kept in a creepy place called the Shadowlands by an evil witch named Sister who was a regular mortal from Outland—the regular world—but gained tremendous magical power by draining it from First Changing Beast. No, no, she wasn't brought there on a quest too, she is the mortal girl that the fairies took nineteen years ago in trade for a fairy changeling, who is my girlfriend, Maggie.

"I saw the number you just punched into your phone—it's the number for the mental hospital—there's really no need for that. How do I know the number? We used to visit Maggie's mother, Mrs. Westerley, there—well, she's the mortal woman who raised Maggie, she's actually Sister's biological mother. Mrs. Westerley is a mean alcoholic who used to beat Maggie, and because the Old Ways of the fairies require symmetry between the changelings, the King of the Fairies used to beat Sister. Oh, yeah, turns out that Maggie is the biological daughter of the King and Queen, so that's who raised Sister. Yes, I totally agree that you'd think if he was King he could change the Old rules, and it was appalling that any of that child abuse occurred, but there you have it. You can imagine how miserable it makes Maggie that all her parents are like that.

"What's that? Her other father? You mean Mr. Westerley, the mortal man who raised her? Well, the Westerleys got divorced when Maggie was real young, and then the King of the Fairies turned Mr. Westerley into a blue stag...look, let's not go there right now.

"The important thing is, Maggie and I found First Changing Beast in the Shadowlands. That's the land between Outland and Inland, so to free it, I have to bring it both places, see, first here, then Inland. But just when we found the Beast, Sister captured Maggie, so it's more urgent than ever that we get back to Inland so I can rescue her.

"Tell those men in the white coats to stay away. Hey, I have a therapist here in town, he'll vouch for me! Dr. Jack Green. Actually, he's Maggie's brother, the Prince of the Fairies. He was a good guy and tried to stop the King from beating Sister after the babies were switched, so the King banished him to Outland and cursed him so he would forget who he is. But once First Changing Beast returns to Inland, Dr. Green can return too... Let me go! Let me go!"

Nope, no good. Better find the Beast as soon as possible.

Dan looked for more tracks. He wished he had a flashlight, but of course he didn't because electricity doesn't work in

Inland or the Shadowlands where he'd just come from, so moonlight would have to do. Most of the ground was grass covered, but Dan figured giant lion paws would leave crushed grass behind. He bent low to peer at the ground as he ran side-to-side, gradually increasing the search arc, but found nothing. How could they disappear this thoroughly? Magic didn't work in Outland, but maybe it made an exception for First Changing Beast.

Blue light pulsed across the ground. It reminded Dan of Inland phosphorescence, but this didn't seem quite right; it was thin, not rich and organic.

"Hey, you!"

Cops for real! Dan had been so absorbed in his search that he hadn't heard the cruiser pull in.

"Hold your hands out where we can see them and walk over here slow-like."

Why were they doing this? Sometimes cops cruised the Goth Woods at night, but they didn't usually hassle anyone who wasn't causing trouble. But as he raised his hands and took a step toward the police, Dan glanced at himself. Crap. He'd forgotten what he looked like: medieval-ish clothing tattered and muddy from pursuing First Changing Beast and Sister in prehistoric Africa, a bulging leather backpack, and worst of all a bow and quiver of arrows. At least the bow was unstrung.

Dan flinched as a bright flashlight caught him full face. "Not that slow. You look a mess. Are those arrows? I think we gotta visit the station with this clown."

"And just when we were having a nice quiet night with nothing to worry about."

Dan had always been a good kid, the kind who obeys cops, so he took a couple more steps toward them. Then he hesitated; this was no time to be that kid. He couldn't afford to spend the

4

night in jail and maybe have them confiscate Breaklock, the amulet that enabled him to travel back and forth between Outland and Inland. Dan couldn't see the cops with the flashlight blaring in his face; all he knew was the first voice had been a man, the second a woman. He hoped they had donut bellies, but even if they were athletes…

Dan turned and bolted. The cops swore and at least one crashed after him. Dan still couldn't see and he jolted into a tree trunk. The cop almost grabbed him but Dan's eyes finally adjusted and he took off again. The cop was fast but Dan was a veteran of long foot journeys and war in Inland, and he wasn't even breathing hard as he zigzagged through the trees and left the pursuit behind.

He paused as the Goth Woods ended at a residential road. Only the man had chased him, so the woman might be coming around in the cruiser. A car drove slowly by, but just a civilian. Dan sprinted across the street, only to hear a siren whoop and see the headlights of a parked police car flash on. Dan cut right, darted down a side street, doubled back through somebody's yard, dodged a dog that woofed its way out of a kennel, scrambled over a wall, and finally cut back to the Goth Woods and crouched in a thicket. A siren faded as the police followed one of his false directions.

Dan sat and thought. He was desperate to rescue Maggie from Sister, but time wasn't as pressing as it would be if all this were happening only in the normal world. He had learned how to aim Breaklock in time, so when he returned to Inland he could get there at exactly the time Maggie had been captured, no matter how long he spent in Outland. That meant he could take as long as necessary to find First Changing Beast. How to find the Beast was another matter. One good thing had come from his encounter with the police: the woman had said it was a quiet night, and Dan was pretty sure she wouldn't have said that if the giant woman and lion were roaming around. First Changing Beast must have taken some less noticeable form. But what?

First things first. Dan couldn't go roaming around Outland unless he took a less noticeable form too. So he'd cut back through the woods and school grounds to his best friend Josh's place, and cross his fingers Josh was home.

* * *

JOSH'S APARTMENT was a couple rooms in the back of his parents' house. Luckily, he had his own entrance, but Dan still approached stealthily. The usual access would be down the driveway, but Dan remembered they had a big motion-activated light there. He sneaked through the yard on the other side of the house, around the back, and up to the door. He raised his hand to tap.

The door flew open and Josh said, "Dude! I knew you'd show up pretty soon. Get inside, you look even worse than usual."

"What do you mean, you knew I'd show up?"

Josh closed the door behind them. "Two words: First. Changing. Beast."

"That's three— It's here?!" Dan stared around and then charged into the bedroom and back out. Plenty of rumpled sheets and clothes on the floor, but no lions or other unusual creatures. "Josh, what are you talking about?"

"Want a beer?"

"No—get away from the frig and tell me why you said First Changing Beast!"

Josh opened the refrigerator door and said, "Let's see: Bud Light, Tecate—oh, how about a freaky statue?"

He turned and held out an ivory statuette less than a foot tall of a humanoid figure with the head of a lion. It looked exactly like the one Dan had seen in the Natural History Museum in New York, itself a reproduction of the original, carved in Germany over 30,000 years ago. It was what First Changing Beast had looked like when Dan first encountered it, except way smaller, of course.

"I don't actually drink much on weeknights because I have the early shift at the Bagel Place," said Josh, "but about an hour ago, just before going to bed, I heard a brewski calling to me loud and clear. Except when I opened the frig, it wasn't a brewski, it was FCB. You want to tell me why it's in my refrigerator, and why I'm up till one a.m. waiting for you?" He handed the statue to Dan. "Oh, by the way, great to see you."

The statue lay still and gray in Dan's hands, to the eye merely a flaky, dry piece of carved ivory. But warmth coursed from it through Dan's hands and up his arms to his chest, and he felt it pulsing in time with his own heart. Dan bear-hugged Josh and said, "This is great! FCB is alive in here. So what happened is—"

Josh's phone binged. He glanced at the screen and turned it to Dan, saying, "And now look what Alice sent."

It was a photo of a prehistoric Venus figurine. Dan had seen one of those in the same museum and recognized it as another avatar of FCB. "Better and better!" he cried. "They're both here!"

"Who both?" asked Josh, his fingers flying over his phone. "Alice already figured out you'd be here. She wants to come hear what's going on, but it's too late for her to be walking around alone. I'll go get her while you shower. And I'll throw your King Arthur stuff in Mom's washing machine. I don't have any clothes to fit you but there's a robe in my bedroom."

* * *

JOSH HAD A BEER AFTER ALL. Alice was only drinking water. She'd brought a travel bag with her, which Dan figured meant she would be spending the night. She and Josh had become a couple on the trip to Inland they took with Dan.

Dan glanced at his backpack. When Alice had handed him the Venus figurine he'd felt the same warmth and vitality he'd felt from the lion person statuette. Both now rested in his backpack, nestled in a towel. Dan took a swig of Diet Coke and began. "Last time I saw you, Josh, I told you Sister's troops were attacking Gatemoodle, right?"

"Yeah. But you were really here to ask Dr. Green about the meaning of Sister's truename so you could use it to control her."

"Minik Mingarria, I already knew it meant the pain she causes people. Dr. Green told me to look into Sister's eyes to learn the other meaning. Well, I got back, and the battle went back and forth, and Sister almost won, when we remembered something Graciela had found out." Their friend Graciela was half-Mayan, and with the help of her shaman father she was the one who learned that the Fairy King had turned Mr. Westerley, the father who raised Maggie, into a blue stag. "Not only that, she was given a horn made out of a piece of his antler that can be used when in great need to call him. Come to think of it, I still have it in my pack. Anyway, I used it and this great blue stag destroyed Sister's army, and in her moment of defeat I looked into her eyes and saw the other meaning of Minik Mingarria: the pain she feels herself."

"So you said it and caught her?" asked Josh.

"She was too quick, gone in a flash. Maggie asked the Fairy King to undo his spell but it turned out the deer didn't want to be changed back. I guess because he has it good as a deer. This gorgeous glowing white doe joined him."

"Poor Maggie!" said Alice. "That was her last chance for a nice parent."

"She's pretty devastated," said Dan. "And it gets worse. Nellie Longarms got killed, and I had to save her."

"If she's already dead you can't save her," said Josh. "I never got what you see in her anyway. I was always kind of turned off by the whole arms-to-her-ankles, aquatic, sharp fangs, probably-eats-children thing."

Dan nodded and shrugged. "But we have a connection. She's helped me and Maggie a lot. I really like her." He'd almost said "love." It wasn't like the way he loved Maggie, but wild Nellie touched the same place deep in his heart that Inland touched. "She really was dead, but I did a spell called Makeless Making, such a powerful spell that it brought her back, but it meant I had to give up something without knowing what. Guess what: it meant I have to leave Inland forever. I only have two months left."

Josh gulped. Alice cried, "Oh, Dan! Inland is what you live for—and Maggie can't survive here; you'll have to leave her too!"

"Luckily, there's a way out," said Dan. "If Maggie and I get married, it cancels that spell and I can stay."

"Isn't there a whole prophecy that you have to get married anyway?" asked Josh.

"Yes. Well, that a mortal and a fairy have to get married, and Maggie and I are the only mortal and fairy couple around. Sister's a mortal, of course, but no one thinks any fairy would marry her. A union between mortal and fairy happens once and only once every five hundred years in Inland; it's a way to strengthen that whole world.

"The King won't let us get married unless I free FCB, but that was my quest anyway. And it's almost done. Maggie and I chased Sister and FCB through the Shadowlands and even into prehistoric Shadowlands as they battled, and finally we were able to get FCB away from her. But at the last minute, Sister truenamed Maggie and escaped with her."

Dan paused. Josh and Alice grimaced and shook their heads. Finally Dan went on, "This was in Africa a million years ago. Don't ask me to explain that, but it's where FCB originated, and maybe because that gave the Beast extra power it became two beings at once: a giant lion and a giant African woman. To free them from the Shadowlands, I had to bring them here first, then to Inland. I brought them here but they disappeared. I think they were smart enough not to wander around Outland as giants, so they became statues and...well, for some reason you have them.

"Now I have to take them to Inland and free Maggie."

"I'm sure you'll save her, Dan," said Alice. "FCB will help, right? Isn't FCB supposed to make everything right in Inland?"

"Yes." Actually, FCB had said something confusing about maybe needing time to get its full power back, but Dan wasn't going to mention that or even think about it; who knew what Sister would do to Maggie, so he needed to rescue her fast, and to be sure of that he needed to believe FCB would make it work.

Josh said, "In this whole crazy story, dude, you didn't mention the other way of stopping Sister: you loving her."

Dan could tell how worried Josh was for him because he didn't waggle his eyebrows or make a stupid joke about him loving Sister. Back when the whole mess happened of the

King of the Fairies cursing the Prince by sending him to Outland (where he eventually became Dr. Green, Dan's therapist), and cursing Mr. Westerley by turning him into a blue deer, the Queen had tried to counter his spell by casting a spell of her own: if someone loved both Maggie and Sister, the daughters would be set free. Well, Dan sure loved Maggie, but…

"Nope. Not gonna happen. Sister's a nightmare." Dan slumped back into his chair. "You know, ever since Sister abducted Maggie I've just been going, going, going. I haven't given myself any time to think about exactly how I'll save Maggie. I can kintravel to her, but what if Sister has monsters right there waiting for me, or what if she forced Maggie to tell her my truename?" Kintravel was an ability that a few people in Inland had to travel instantaneously to someone they loved. "I'm counting a lot on FCB."

"You'll have other help, too," said Alice.

"What do you mean?"

"Josh and I are going back with you."

"I don't think—"

"Two words," interrupted Josh. "Listen. Up."

"Why do you think FCB magically came to Josh and me?" asked Alice.

"I've been too busy to think about it," answered Dan, "but I guess they knew you would keep them safe for me."

"That's stupid," said Josh. "They could have just materialized in your pack and you could have zipped right back to Inland with them."

"It's obvious," said Alice. "They came to us as a message that we are to go back with you."

"Are you forgetting last time?" asked Dan. Josh and Alice had had enough of Inland on their last trip—too many times being almost slain by goblin-like creatures, almost eaten by wolves, threatened by a dragon...

Josh and Alice looked at each other and nodded. "We sure haven't forgotten," answered Josh. "And we're scared. But something big is going on, and FCB wants us to be part of it, and we're your best friends."

Alice held up her travel bag. "I know Billy and the other Gatekeepers will have clothes for us, but some things Inland doesn't do very well. I already packed underwear, toilet paper, and toothbrush."

Dan laughed, first about Alice's wise planning, and then about the idea of them coming with him. "I'm not going to argue anymore," he said. "It will be great to have you along. I would have needed to come get you soon to be our Best Man and Maid of Honor, anyway." *If* he rescued Maggie so they could get married, that is. Dan pushed that thought out of his mind.

"OK, and here's our first help," said Josh. "Bring Jack Green."

"He's not allowed back in Inland until...oh, right." The Fairy Queen had also countered the King's curse by making it so their son could return to Outland once First Changing Beast was free. "But why bring him now?"

"Because he helps you figure things out," said Josh.

"Do you have any idea at all where Sister has Maggie?" asked Alice.

"Well—no."

"There you go," said Josh. "And anyway, how will Green get back if you don't bring him?"

"I don't know," said Dan. He had trouble thinking about all this. It was probably because of what Dr. Green called transference. Dan had a ton of respect for Dr. Green as someone who helped him, and it was hard to imagine switching things around and instead him being the one who helped Dr. Green by taking him back to his heritage as Prince of the Fairies. "Anyway, that would be a terrible thing to yank him away from his other patients and they never see him again."

"But they can see him again," said Alice. "With FCB, the Gates of Inland will be open. Dr. Green can return and close down his practice properly. And he can return right when he leaves, right?"

"We're for sure counting on you working that time trick," said Josh. "We want to help you save Maggie, be there for the wedding and a whopdoodle party, and then you bring us back right now so we don't lose our jobs and freak out our families."

"Maybe you're right," said Dan. "Dr. Green was famous among the fairies for exploring all over, studying the land and the animals, so he'd know likely places for Sister to take Maggie if anyone would. Plus he's blood relations with Maggie and adoptive relations with Sister, so he might have some weird Inland feel for where they are." Maybe it was just Dan's old trust in Dr. Green as his therapist, but he suddenly felt a lot more optimistic.

"Except I don't know how we could get him to go with us."

"Can't you just explain things to him?" asked Alice.

Dan shook his head. "I tried to tell him he was Prince of the Fairies last time I talked to him. The curse is too strong. He literally didn't hear a single word I said on the subject."

"Then you need my and Alice's help again already," said Josh. "We'll figure out a plan. In fact, it seems obvious: We go over there at the end of his workday, as he's coming out you make a gate and we shove him through."

"Uh, no," said Dan. "Even if that would work, and I'm not sure it would because the timing would have to be perfect.

We're not going to muscle my therapist around. He's my *therapist*, show some respect."

"But it would be for his own good, back to fairyland where he's Prince," protested Josh.

"No."

"If he can't hear anything about being a Prince, could you just tell him what Inland is like?" asked Alice. "Persuade him to go just because it's so wonderful?"

"That won't work either," said Dan. "Therapists don't go places with their patients because if they did it would just turn into a regular relationship instead of one where you can tell them everything. Besides, Inland can't be captured in words." Dan had tried sometimes: In Inland the colors were richer, the air sweeter, the wind like music, waves like song, sun shining scintillating gems, moon a coal of cool rapture, flowers ringing like gongs, and foods with flavors simple and exotic at the same time, a phosphorescent sensory tangle.

"But that gives me an idea!" said Dan. "If words won't do it, maybe music will."

"What, like have Josh sing and he'll jump through a gate to Inland just to escape?" asked Alice.

Dan laughed. "Soon after baby Maggie was switched for baby Sister, and Mrs. Westerley started hating on Maggie, Dr. Green—you know, when he was Prince of the Fairies—made a stuffed rabbit and a rattle and brought them to Maggie. Mrs. Westerley eventually made Maggie watch as she cut up the rabbit—"

"Oh! Why?" asked Alice.

Dan shrugged. "Because Mrs. Westerley. She tried to smash the rattle too, but Maggie hid it. If I can find that rattle and we rattle it for Dr. Green I bet it will start reminding him of Inland. Rattleman, remember?" That creepy name had been whispered to Dan a while back and his friends had helped him figure out it was a nickname for Dr. Green. "Even as an Outland psychologist he has a collection of artistic rattles in his office, so he still has a special feeling about them, and this rattle will be extra special because it's from Inland and from him too. So he'll feel a connection that may draw him in. Then we go through the gate and hope he follows.

"My clothes should be dry by now, and there's still a few hours of darkness. I'm going to do this little B & E on my own, so if I get caught you won't be charged as accomplices." And mainly because Josh and Alice would slow him down. "Just lend me a flashlight."

"Mrs. Westerley is still gone?" asked Alice.

"Yep." When she had found out that Sister was the biological daughter she had lost, Mrs. Westerley had followed her into Inland. "In fact, she and Sister seem to actually be getting along. They travel together and Sister keeps her safe. So the house will be empty."

* * *

As Dan had hoped, a downstairs window was unlocked. Mrs. Westerley seemed much happier now that she was in Inland with Sister, but she had spent most of her time here drunk and angry. A quick glance to make sure the neighborhood was asleep, and Dan pushed up the window and slipped inside.

The odor of moldy, unlaundered sheets enveloped him. He flashed the light on a rumpled bed covered with a jumble of clothes he didn't want to look at closely. This must be Mrs. Westerley's bedroom. He took a step and kicked something that clinked as it fell over. After listening to make sure there were no answering sounds outside, Dan shone his light down to reveal an empty gin bottle. He flashed the light around to find the doorway, and the beam caught a baby photo on the dresser. Dan stepped closer and picked it up. Babies all looked alike and Dan didn't know much about them, but he was pretty sure this was a hospital photo of a newborn, which meant it was Sister.

An ache stronger than the stench of bedsheets struck Dan. Poor Mrs. Westerley! He hated her for the way she had treated Maggie, but was it really her fault? The fairies had randomly taken away her actual baby, and she knew it somehow, and ever since she'd only wanted her own baby back. Dr. Green—well, the Fairy Prince—tried to make it better but his father found out and stopped him because the stupid Old Ways required the baby they'd taken to Inland to be treated the same way as the baby they'd left in Outland; rather than stopping Mrs. Westerley's abuse of Maggie, they had to abuse Sister. Anyway, Mrs. Westerley had somehow become aware of Dr. Green and called him a scary Rattleman. Maybe he'd just made things worse. Dan didn't like thinking that about his therapist so he put the photo back and found his way out of the bedroom.

It abutted the kitchen, and from there Dan knew his way up the stairs to Maggie's room. He stepped inside and wondered, "Now what?" It was a small room with a small closet, so not many places to hide things, but he didn't want to go rooting through Maggie's drawers like a pervert. Besides, Mrs. Westerley had probably rooted through any of the obvious places many times in a drunken rage.

Dan turned on the flashlight and a demon leered at him. He dropped the light and jumped back, thudding against the wall. As the light rolled on the floor, bloody skulls and vampires seemed to lunge out. But the flashlight came to a stop and the creatures froze. Wall art! Dan breathed heavily, shone the light once all around the room, and turned it off.

He'd only been in this room once before. That was after their first trip to Inland, and they had made love on this bed, and then Maggie told Dan she could never see him again unless he took her to Inland. They hadn't yet learned Maggie was a fairy, but after experiencing Inland she knew she couldn't survive in Outland any longer. Before Dan discovered her true nature and helped her back to Inland she had attempted suicide. It must have been around then that she painted her walls.

Minik Mingarria indeed! So much pointless pain. How could a place as marvelous as Inland hurt people so much? How could ancient, wondrous fairies and the ancient, wondrous landscape in which they dwelt be linked with static Old Ways and child abuse? Dan felt the world bulging with more things in it than he could imagine, good, bad, and a lot of them just there. How did anyone find their way?

A siren broke Dan's reverie. A siren getting louder. Either his flashlight or that bump against the wall must have alerted neighbors. Right now all he had to do was find the rattle and find it quick, Step One in rescuing Maggie. But how?

The paintings told him. All around the room they snarled and glared and threatened, except in the corner by the bed. Heedless now of any sound he made, Dan yanked the bed from the wall, knelt, and began pounding. The wall was solid, but a floorboard thunked loosely. Dan tore it aside and stuck his hand in the hole, praying no vermin. The siren had stopped and Dan figured that meant they were close, approaching silently so as not to scare him off. He touched something soft, and then something hard that rattled. He grabbed the rattle and shoved it in his pocket, then hesitated as he was about to leap down the stairs. He reached back for the soft thing, hoping it wasn't some gross bug. He pulled it out and stared a moment, baffled, then smiled and charged downstairs. It was the ear of Maggie's stuffed bunny that her mother had cut to pieces when she was a child. Maggie would want that. He sprinted through Mrs. Westerley's bedroom and a spotlight hit him just as he dove through the open window. When he rolled to his feet, a familiar voice shouted, "It's that same kid!"

Well, he knew he was faster than them. Dan exulted in his muscles and lungs and exulted that he was on the cusp of triumph. Who cares if they found his fingerprints in the house? He was about to free First Changing Beast, and about to find out how to rescue Maggie and deal with Sister once and for all, and the cops couldn't follow him to Inland.

DAN, Josh, and Alice sat in Dr. Green's waiting room. He had looked surprised and probably a little angry (Dan hoped he was imagining that) when he had opened the outer door in response to their buzz, but before going back to his inner office he'd merely said, "I'm with my last patient of the day. Have a seat, all of you."

"Remember," whispered Dan, "I'll start talking to him as soon as he opens the door, and Alice, you start rattling. There's a painting in his office that's actually a road and gate in Inland, though for sure Dr. Green doesn't realize that anymore. But a long time ago when I challenged him about Inland, and he told me he can't talk about it, the picture cracked. Something about the curse being intensified if Green starts to remember Inland. So if the rattle works, the painting should at least wobble a little and maybe even crack. Josh, you be watching and tell me if that happens. That'll mean Green is thinking of Inland and I'll make the gate then. I'm going to make it open at Gatemoodle so we can consult with Billy Portman and the other Gatekeepers. I have to go through first with the statues, because the curse says Green can only return to Inland after FCB. You guys come right away whether Green does or not, because the gates don't last long."

"What if it doesn't work?" asked Alice.

Dan frowned. "Then somehow we find Maggie without him —look, this has to work."

The minutes poked by. Dan said, "Oh, there's a different exit for patients, so be ready: it'll be Dr. Green who comes out here."

Almost as soon as Dan said that, the door opened and Dr. Green leaned out.

Dan hopped up and said, "Dr. Green, I am so sorry to impose on you like this. Oh, these are my friends Josh and Alice, I've told you about them. I'm about to make a gate to Inland for all of us to go through." Alice began shaking the rattle. "I know I'm just babbling," babbled Dan, and then stopped. Whether the rattle was affecting Dr. Green or not, Dan felt calm and restful.

Dr. Green glanced at the rattle, then back at Dan. "Would you like to come into my office?"

Alice shook the rattle harder. Dr. Green frowned and looked at her, and Dan thought he saw a gleam in his eye. Then Green shook his head and said, "Come on in."

"Let's listen a little more. This rattle doesn't look like much but it's even fancier than the ones in your display case."

Dr. Green looked at Dan, somehow smiling and frowning at the same time. He looked at the rattle, irregularly carved but glossy with the browns and tans of an old tree knot. He raised his eyebrows. Alice rattled louder. Josh said, "Dan, it's moving!" and suddenly there was a loud snap and splinters of glass struck the floor.

Dan took out Breaklock and did the gate-making ritual. The

green portal shimmered in front of him. Dan said, "Come with us, Dr. Green," and stepped through. Josh and Alice were right behind him.

The gate flared and then began to fade. Just before it blinked out, Dr. Green strode beside them. He breathed in deeply, smiled, and looked at the old rustic Hall.

"The Prince of the Fairies has many things to talk about with old Billy," he said. Then he looked at Dan. "But how can I aid you? You are the mover of things now."

# GATE MUDDLE

*D*an took a deep breath of Inland air that felt like fresh cold water at the end of a desert hike. Only a few days earlier the ground here had been churned and the foliage destroyed in Sister's war, yet no scars remained. Trees waved to him in a warm breeze, the turf was thick with grass and flowers, and thrushes and cardinals sang melody to the background rhythm of bees and grasshoppers. Even as Dan watched, the flowers swelled, their hues grew richer, and the birdsong sweeter. He patted his backpack and smiled; FCB was working magic already.

Then from behind came staccato banging. Dan turned and saw an old oak raising a dead spar to the sky, and on that spar stood a great woodpecker, gorgeously patterned in red, black, and white. It banged again, pulled a grub lunch from the hole, and stared at Dan as it swallowed the fat, wriggling creature. Yuck! A worm in the core of Inland? Dan looked back at the flowers to push that thought away.

A louder bang came from the hilltop: the door of Gatemoodle Hall itself slamming shut. The woodpecker flew away as the Gatekeepers—Billy Portman, Mother Ferny, and Crackerbones—ran down the hill, followed by Graciela. Graciela hugged them but the Gatekeepers stopped short. When Dan stepped back from Graciela, he saw that they were staring at Dr. Green.

Billy bowed to Dan's old therapist and said, "Greetings, Prince. Welcome back to the wide world."

Dr. Green returned the bow and said, "Greetings to you Billy, and Mother Ferny, and Crackerbones too. I do not doubt that you have worked much good for Inland in my absence. I hope to learn from you how things now stand."

The Gatekeepers turned and stared at Dan. Just as it was starting to get uncomfortable, they all bowed to him and Billy said, "You have rewarded our trust in you Dan. You have freed First Changing Beast. We know this because under the terms of his father's curse the Prince could not return to Inland otherwise. Yet..."

Billy trailed off and Mother Ferny took over. "We do not perceive a difference. Neither earth nor air tells a tale of First Changing Beast's return."

Billy turned and asked Dr. Green, "Could there be any doubt about the curse?"

"None," said Dr. Green.

"Then returned the Beast surely is," said Billy. "If the expected tendrils of freedom were spreading, the dwarves and allied goblins and other friends would already be making preparations to journey here. As it is we will send out messages and it will take some days before all can assemble, but then we shall have a feast such as our old Hall has not seen in a thousand years! Yet Maggie is not with you, so the story you have to tell is not entirely happy, and maybe there are deeds yet to do. Come inside and explain over a simple meal."

"I would love one of your meals, Billy, but there's no time," said Dan. "You are right that there are deeds to do: Sister true-named Maggie and carried her away! I took First Changing Beast to Outland and returned here at exactly the minute Sister captured her, but I don't like Maggie being under truenaming even for a moment." Dan had seen Maggie truenamed, and experienced it himself; it was hard even to find words for that cold despair, that abject enslavement that felt eternal even seconds after it began. "I need to rescue her now." Dan patted his pack and thought, "With FCB's help."

But Billy and Mother Ferny shook their heads. Dr. Green said, "Hard as it is, it is better for Maggie to suffer a little longer while you tell us the tale and we help you plan, than for you to rush to her and fail."

Mother Ferny added, "Even though we have not forgotten the other reason to hurry: you and Maggie must wed so you are not banished forever from Inland."

"That's a second-place reason now," said Dan, pacing side to side. "I still have almost two months for that, but Maggie might go mad if I leave her truenamed that long."

"Still," said Alice, putting her hand on his shoulder. "A plan."

So once again Dan found himself seated at the scarred wooden table in Gatemoodle. Sometimes he had sat there to partake of Billy Portman's delicious cooking, sometimes to participate in councils about the fate of Inland, and sometimes, like now, to do both. He spread butter on a slab of crusty bread still warm from the old wood-burning stove and spooned up a mouthful of thick potato soup. He had long ago given up on trying to figure out how Billy could have meals freshly prepared for Dan's random arrivals.

Yet somehow now it felt different. Dan gazed around the table and thought it must be partly because of just who had assembled this time. Maggie was missing of course. And Alice was here for the first time, a Gatemoodle stop not being part of her previous trip to Inland. She had squeezed into a seat between Josh and Graciela and avoided eye contact with the Gatekeepers across the table. Dan couldn't blame her. Billy was fine, even though he was a hobgoblin—more than fine, he gave off the aura of a genial little grandfather, although the creases in his face and the depth of his eyes suggested more wisdom than was attainable during a mortal lifespan. But Mother Ferny was a witch, and although Dan knew her to be a healer and a fierce protector, at first glance she looked Halloween-scary, with wild black and silver hair, prominent hooked nose, and black cloak and dress. And Crackerbones...Crackerbones had the sharp teeth, blotchy green skin, and lank hair of a goblin. It was only because the old wooden beams of Gatemoodle were saturated with spells of amity that a hobgoblin, a witch, and a goblin could serve together as Gatekeepers to preserve as much as possible the passages between Inland and Outland. But the spells of amity hadn't stopped Crackerbones from being hostile to Dan and his friends. At least, now that Dan had succeeded in the quest the Gatekeepers had set him to free First Changing Beast, he would probably stop threatening to eat Dan.

Graciela whispered something to Alice, probably reassurance, because Alice looked up and smiled at Billy and Mother Ferny. That was like Graciela: not real effusive, but strong and competent. She had stayed at Gatemoodle after helping defend it in the war with Sister's troops. She saw Dan looking at her and winked.

And of course Dr. Green had never been at Gatemoodle with Dan, although it was obvious that he had some old connection with the Gatekeepers. Dr. Green...Dan wondered if he could even call him "Dr. Green" anymore. And he realized that was another part of what felt different. When he'd first consulted Dr. Green he'd been an angsty high school kid, bored about going to college and getting some stupid job, scared he'd never find a girlfriend. But ever since Billy Portman first contacted Dan his life had been unimaginably exciting, and not only did he have a girlfriend, his girlfriend was a fairy princess. So he didn't really need a therapist anymore. Still...even with his exciting, fulfilling life, things weren't easy, and he'd enjoyed checking in with Dr. Green now and then. Even if he'd never gone for another therapy session, just the idea that he *could* go was comforting. But now he couldn't anymore, not really.

Dan took another bite of bread and spooned up more soup. There was another difference, too: Things were ending. Ending in a good way, of course. He had freed First Changing Beast, and with the Beast's help it should be easy enough to defeat Sister and rescue Maggie. Then would come their wedding day, and Dan would be free to come and go from Inland as he chose. But still...ending.

The woodpecker broke his reverie, banging away again loud enough to hear through the thick walls. Dan pictured the gray branch behind its bright colors. He pushed his food away.

"I would be very anxious if First Changing Beast weren't free," said Dan. "But the Beast will set things right, right? Here's what happened." He described how he and Maggie had rescued FCB, adding, "There's one part I didn't mention, uh, for some reason, when I told you guys, Josh and Alice. FCB said that when Maggie and I get married it will be a double wedding, uh..."

Josh and Alice started laughing. "Not us, dude," said Josh.

Alice poked him in the chest but said, "We are nowhere close to that, Dan."

Dan shrugged. "Who knows what they meant, then. But what planning do we need to do? Together with First Changing Beast it will be easy to defeat Sister, won't it?"

"Where is the Beast?" asked Crackerbones. "Why can we not feel it? Where is the Beast?"

Dan knew exactly where the Beast was, so he hadn't let the Gatekeepers' concern about the absent "tendrils of freedom" bother him. He'd kept his pack right beside him instead of hanging it on the usual peg by the entrance, and now he unzipped it and reached inside. And frowned and bent to look as he pushed aside clothes, snacks, water bottles, first-aid kit, and the little horn that could magically summon the blue stag. He dumped everything on the floor and tossed it around, finally putting his head in his hands and groaning, dimly aware of the sounds of Crackerbones tapping claws on table and Mother Ferny whispering to Billy.

"I should have known," muttered Dan.

"That First Changing Beast is not the luggage?" asked Crackerbones. "Yes, yes, you should have known."

Dan let Josh and Alice explain about the statues. He was too busy spinning his mind around the idea that FCB had changed again so he was going to have to rescue Maggie without its help.

Crackerbones sneered and rolled his eyes, but Mother Ferny said, "Do not be too alarmed, Dan. It is not in First Changing Beast's nature to willingly spend time in confinement, whether in the Shadowlands from which you rescued it, or in your back-pack in which you carried it, or in statues where it bided in Outland. After so much time trapped in the Shadowlands and bled by Sister, First Changing Beast may need to recuperate in some secure den."

Dan nodded. "The woman and lion told me they weren't at full strength and might not be until the wedding. I just thought they'd be strong enough to give some help." He sighed and stood up. "Then there's no point in talking any longer. I can't delay while FCB gathers its strength. Maggie is suffering, and I have to free her. I bet Sister has forced Maggie to tell her my truename by now, so give me something to plug my ears—Mother Ferny, I bet you can make something herbal that will block all sound. Then I kintravel to Maggie, find Sister—shouldn't be hard, she's probably lurking to capture me—truename her, and force her to release Maggie. While I'm at it I'll force her to stop ruining Inland."

"That plan is bold but not wise--" began Billy.

Dan interrupted. "There's no time to argue. If Mother Ferny won't help with earplugs I'll find something else." He strode over to the shelves.

"Dude!" said Josh. "When he said 'not wise' that was polite hobgoblin talk for 'a few fries short of a Happy Meal.' These guys live here full-time, let's listen to them."

"They live here full-time but they've never been truenamed and they don't know how much it hurts," said Dan, sorting through weird pieces of bark, rock, and fabric, none of which looked like earplug material.

"Sister will have anticipated your intent to kintravel to her," said Billy. "So she will have taken Maggie into the Marrowland, where you'll remember the King has made kintravel impossible."

Dan knew it was true as soon as he heard it. He dropped a hunk of amber and plodded back to the table as Dr. Green said, "My father has forbidden kintravel?"

"Yes, so Sister could not readily attack him."

Dr. Green shook his head. "Protecting himself from his own adoptive daughter. Such a mess he has made."

"But Dan, we do understand the urgency," said Billy. "Perhaps First Changing Beast will recuperate rapidly enough to help. As you know, we have a gate through which we pass from time to time to gather Outland food. I will read our gate for news of First Changing Beast."

"Huh?" said Dan.

"Hey, even I understand that," said Josh. "Ever since you first got involved with Inland it's been all about 'First Changing Beast will keep the gates open.' So no surprise, the gates can feel him."

"Indeed," said Billy, with a nod to Josh. "I do not expect to be long."

Dan had never known where the Gatemoodle gate was, so watching Billy was enough to take his mind off Maggie for a moment. The hobgoblin walked to a spot in the middle of the Hall next to the woodburning stove, knelt, and passed his hands over the smooth floorboards. A rope handle appeared where nothing had been before, and when Billy pulled on it a trapdoor opened with an old-root-cellar creak. Billy was wiry and a foot shorter than Dan, but even so the opening looked way too small. As Dan ran over for a closer look, Billy jumped over the edge and appeared to shrink as he dropped into the hole. Dan gazed into a narrow vertical earthen passage, the rope attached to one side quivering as Billy disappeared into the darkness. The trapdoor closed unassisted.

At any other time, Dan would have been delighted by the weirdness of Billy's departure. As it was, he wandered back to the table and slouched in his chair.

"No matter how much time I have, I cannot make earplugs

that will block Sister's voice if she speaks a truename with all her power," said Mother Ferny.

"Worse and worse," groaned Dan.

"I can help, Dan," said Dr. Green.

"Thanks, Dr. Green, but as much as your therapy has done for me, this isn't the time. This is the time for action. But if FCB can't help, it's going to take forever to rescue Maggie. The Marrowland is huge, and I don't know where to start."

"I agree that it is time for action. And I agree that the Marrowland is huge. But before my banishment I explored it from the Ice Sky Mountains in the north to the Crawling Desert in the south, from the Lagoons of Longing in the East to the Blossom Jungle in the West. No one knows the Marrowland better than I. Let us put our heads together and see if we can figure out what kind of place Sister is likely to choose for her lair, and then I will guide you there if First Changing Beast cannot."

"That's great if you can do that," said Dan. "That's the first bit of good news since we got here. But do you mean we should think about what kind of person Sister is and use that to figure out what kind of place she'd choose to hide in? I'm not sure any of us know her that well. Mean Person Central? Sorry, I'm too worried to think."

"And I have not known her since she was a toddler, so any ideas will need to come from the rest of you," said Dr. Green.

"Hmmm," said Graciela. "She's not only mean, she's arrogant. When we took her to New York City she decided to look like a fancy rich Upper East Sider, and yes, fancy rich Upper East Siders can be perfectly nice, but in Sister it just reinforced her attitude that she's above everyone else. Does that get us anywhere? She'll insist on someplace fancy, away from anything common? At least we can be sure she won't try to hide by blending in with commoners."

After a pause, Josh said, "She used to have a fancy moving palace not far from the Marrowland. But it makes no sense that she'd use that if she's trying to stay hidden."

Then came a longer pause. Dan felt even more discouraged; this was going nowhere. He looked at the furrowed brows of his friends and watched Josh and Alice whisper for a while. Then he noticed that Mother Ferny and Crackerbones had left the table to stand, arms crossed, staring at where the trapdoor had disappeared.

"Hey, Mother Ferny, is something wrong?" called Dan. "Should Billy be back already?"

"Oh, I'm sure all is fine," answered the witch. "Just to read the gate takes little time, but Billy probably went on through to gather some food. You have enough to worry about trying to figure out where Sister is. Don't worry about Billy."

That was totally not reassuring, so it was a relief when Alice called out, "We have an idea! The one good thing we accomplished with that New York episode was getting Sister together with her birth mother, Mrs. Westerley. Sister was really mean to her when they met, but later in the fancy castle she was taking care of her mother like she meant something to her. We aren't getting anywhere thinking about Sister, so we should think about Mrs. Westerley!"

Dan sat up straighter, and Graciela said, "That is a good idea! When Sister came to the war, she brought her mother along and was totally solicitous. I bet wherever she is, she has Mrs. Westerley there to take care of her."

"And by 'we have an idea,' Alice meant 'Alice has an idea,'" said Josh, smiling at her. "The main thing I know about Mrs.

Westerley is she's an alcoholic. Any gin factories in the Marrowland? Any place where gin bottles grow on trees?"

"She's lost weight," said Dan. "I think her time in Inland has cured her alcoholism." Still, something about what Josh said reminded him of something.

As he tried to focus on it, Dan heard a prolonged creak. Crackerbones had the trapdoor open and was saying, "Do not be absurd, Mother Ferny. It is much harder for you than I to fit, and goblins are made for dark tunnels." Crackerbones jumped into the hole, shrinking like Billy had. The trapdoor closed behind him.

"Don't tell us not to worry now, Mother Ferny," said Dan. "What's going on?"

"Perhaps Billy brought back too much food to carry," replied Mother Ferny. "He does like to be able to make good meals for us. Cracker has just gone to help."

Could Billy really be in serious trouble? Dan had seen him handle so many hazardous situations with a smile. He met Dr. Green's eyes.

"All we can do is complete the task we have to do," said Dr. Green. "A moment ago you looked like you were having a thought. What was it?"

"Something Josh said…when he wondered about gin bottle trees…trees, that's it! When Maggie and I chased Sister through the Shadowlands, following her to First Changing Beast, for a long time the places we went were a mixture of our minds and Sister's mind. The Gatekeepers had told us that the Shadowlands come in part from the minds of whoever is there, and since Maggie and I and Sister had entwined tasks, the Shadowlands came from all of us. OK, with me so far?" Josh rolled his eyes. "Anyway, Mrs. Westerley appeared as a witch in a Gingerbread house. The thing is, on a different trip Maggie and I had been walking through that same forest in Inland—not the Shadowlands, but regular Inland—and we passed a sign for 'Gingerbread House,' so that's what was in Maggie's and my minds. Then when we were in what looked like the same woods but in the Shadowlands, the sign didn't say 'Gingerbread House,' it said 'Woods Witch.' So that must have come from Sister's mind! She's with Mrs. Westerley in a woods!" Then Dan's voice sank. "But there's probably tons of woods in the Marrowland."

"Anything else you remember about that particular woods?" asked Dr. Green.

"Well, yeah, I guess." Dan stood up. "There was a vulture named Piebald, one of the Woods Witch's familiars. It was black except for a big white ruff below its bald head and neck."

Dr. Green smiled. "Now we are getting somewhere. The White-Ruffed Vulture is a southern species. But there are still many woodlands in the south; do you remember anything else?"

Dan sat back down and drummed his fingers. "No."

"I know you feel very pressured, but give yourself a moment," said Dr. Green. "Just see what comes to mind."

Dan smiled. Even if Green was a prince he was still a therapist. "OK then… Her other familiar was a black cat the size of a beagle, but I don't suppose that helps. Wasn't a wildcat or anything… The familiars had names, Piebald and Pyewocket, and they could talk. They wanted to kill me and Maggie, but Mrs. W wouldn't let them, in fact she was kind of nice to us and they were mean to her about that…and they made fun of her for caring about her daughters…and they made fun of her because she was obsessed with rattles."

"Sure, because of the Rattleman," said Josh. "She was going

on about him even back in the psych ward back home. The Rattleman, ha, that's you, Dr. Green."

"Indeed," said Dr. Green. "And now we are really getting somewhere. Although none of the Marrowland trees grow gin, in the south there is an entire woodland—"

The trapdoor lifted, so fast this time that the creak sounded more like a scream. Crackerbones popped out but held the trap open.

"Quickly, Mother!" he cried. "His regular catnip does not suffice. He faces a cruel one the size of a beagle. Conjure a special blend!"

"Pyewocket!" shouted Dan. "What's going on?"

Mother Ferny ignored him as she ran to her spice cabinet, instead calling, "Bring me a fabric square." Dan darted for the shelves as she pulled pale green leaves from one canister and dried yellow flowers from another. Crushing them together, she said, "An hour would strengthen it, Cracker."

"A minute may be too long!"

Mother Ferny frowned and added two pinches of something red as Dan handed her the bit of cloth he had seized. She folded the wad into the fabric, pulled needle and thread from thin air, sealed it with a few fast stitches, and tossed the ball to Crackerbones. He disappeared into the hole and the lid slammed shut.

"Now can you tell us what is going on?" asked Dan.

Mother Ferny walked to where the trapdoor disappeared and held her hand out in the pushing-away gesture. "I must concentrate," she said.

Dan plodded back to the table and sat watching Mother Ferny watching for the trapdoor to open. Graciela cleared her throat and said, "We might as well hear Dr. Green's idea."

"What?" Dan kept looking at the trapdoor space. "Uh, sure."

"As I was saying," resumed Dr. Green, "in the south there is an entire woodland of trees that grow gourd-sized seedpods that rattle in the slightest breeze. The Chattertree Woods."

"Huh. I guess that helps a little," said Dan. "Since Mrs. Westerley is terrified of the Rattleman, a woods that reminded her of him would be the last place she'd want to be, so we can rule that one out. But then there's your Blossom Jungle and how many other forests, too?"

"I am confident at least that she will avoid the dangerous Blossom Jungle," said Dr. Green. "And I'm not at all sure that she'll avoid the Chattertree Woods. Mrs. Westerley knew something was off as soon as my father switched Maggie for Sister, and right away she began yelling at Maggie and treating her roughly. I wanted to soothe baby Maggie, both for her sake and so Father would stop abusing Sister to create balance in the Old Ways. And so I visited baby Maggie with enchanted rattles to calm and cheer her, and she would laugh and coo. But I wasn't as skilled at hiding as I should have been, nor had I yet learned enough psychology to understand that to heal a broken mother-child bond it is as necessary to heal the mother as to heal the child. When Mrs. Westerley glimpsed me she must have thought I was something out of a ghost story. 'Rattleman' indeed! And so I fear that I truly traumatized Mrs. Westerley. That is my contribution to the tangle of disaster that we are trying to sort out."

Dr. Green sighed. "Be that as it may, our task now is to learn from it what we can. People's reactions to trauma are not straightforward. As you say, Dan, many want to avoid any reminder. But other trauma victims seek out ways to re-experience the trauma, in dream life and even in waking life, in hopes that the new version will work out better and they can master their fears."

"The familiars said something like that!" broke in Dan.

"They said that whenever Mrs. W was going on about rattles they couldn't tell if it was because rattles scared her or made her calmer."

"There you have it," said Dr. Green. "Then our best guess is that Maggie is the captive of Sister and Mrs. Westerley in the Chattertree Woods. Nothing is certain, but I think that is enough to go on. We will try to kintravel to Maggie, and that will take us to the border of the Marrowland that is nearest her. If we are in the vicinity of the Chattertree Woods, our guess is confirmed."

"And if not?" asked Graciela.

The trapdoor screeched and banged open before Dr. Green could answer. Crackerbones hopped out, then reached down the hole and Billy followed, half on his own power and half with Crackerbones's assist. Billy was breathing heavily and his trousers and shirtsleeves were shredded. One arm bled where claws had raked it. He slumped into one of the easy chairs behind the table. Mother Ferny was quickly beside him with ointments and bandages.

Dan and his friends all clamored to ask what had happened and if they could help. It was Crackerbones who answered—Crackerbones without his usual sarcasm. "Billy and his kind have been visiting homes and raiding pantries forever. Hiding from old people is simple, but not so hiding from babies and pets. Babies like seeing them—you may have heard mothers laugh when their little ones stare into space that they are seeing fairies, little knowing that it is true. Cats and dogs are a greater challenge, but hobs know ways to pass them safely. Billy has never had a problem."

Billy took over, rubbing his freshly bandaged arm. "This was no ordinary cat. It was of great size, but that was only a problem because it was coupled with great malice. Sister had set this cat to guard our gate. Mother, thank you for the herbs; my attacker will sleep for some time now. But our gate is no longer safe to use."

"No more Outland food?" asked Alice.

"For now," answered Billy. "But that is of small import. I went to read the gate, and it has given messages not only from First Changing Beast but from Sister also. The gate tells me that Sister has a new kind of power. Although Dan rescued First Changing Beast so that Sister no longer can drain him in the Shadowlands, in her long use of him she established a frail lattice of his power at her core. On this lattice she now sculpts power that she draws from Maggie. She claims that twinning makes her greater than whole. Dan, we already knew you needed to rescue Maggie for her own sake, and that was more than reason enough. But now I know that in saving her you will be taking one step toward saving Inland."

"Sister always talked about how she and Maggie had a connection and it would be great to join with Maggie," said Dan quietly. "If not sisters of blood, she said once, they were sisters of bone. I guess that's what she means by twinning. But what does she mean by greater than whole, and how does she sculpt power from that?"

"A version of that occurs even in Outland," explained Dr. Green. "People who feel themselves to be fragmented, split, alone and alienated, feel completed and empowered if they find a partner who seems like another version of them. They feel safe in a world that they now experience in their own image. But it is a fragile solution, dissolved if the psychological twin leaves."

Dan shrugged. "OK, whatever. So saving Maggie will be saving Inland, but like you say, Billy, I was going to save her anyway. But what did you mean by saying I would be taking 'one step'? That sounds like there's gonna be more steps, and I don't want more steps."

"A second step is needed, both steps to be taken quickly."

Dan stood up from the table. "I've been saying all along I need to save Maggie quickly. So let's quit stalling!"

"Already it is evening," said Dr. Green. "It will not be safe to kintravel and arrive during the night. We leave at dawn. Let us hear why Billy says there is new reason to hurry."

Billy nodded. "As we told you long ago, Dan, a person who lives their life intensely in a new way may grow into a new truename. The longer that Sister sculpts a new self by twinning with Maggie, the greater the chance that her truename will change."

Dan's only weapon against Sister was her truename. He slumped back into his chair.

When he was able to tune in again, he heard Mother Ferny asking, "What is Dan's second step? And what message did you read in the gate from First Changing Beast?"

"To answer one question is to answer the other," replied Billy. "The gate tells me that the Beast has been rescued physically but not in spirit. I am sorry Dan. I know you do not like this idea. But more than ever I think that your rescue of the Beast from the Shadowlands, the Land Between, must be infused with love that passes between the lands, Outland and Inland both. It finally explains why we knew to choose you for the task. Already you love Maggie who was born in Inland and raised in Outland. But that is not enough. You must also love the one who was born in Outland and raised in Inland. You must love Sister."

Long ago the Queen of the Fairies, Maggie's birth mother, Sister's adoptive mother, had cast a spell that if one person could love both women they would be freed of their torment.

Dan had hoped that Mrs. Westerley's husband—Sister's birth father, Maggie's adoptive father—could fulfill the task, but he had been turned into a blue stag that was in love with a beautiful white doe. Dan had imagined that Maggie's best Outland friend, the Green Goblin, was weird and creative enough for the task, but the Green Goblin had turned him down. And in fact, the Queen herself had told Dan that she thought he was the one. But...

"I cannot possibly imagine how to love someone as cruel as Sister," said Dan. "She's pretty sometimes, but that just makes her the poster girl for Looks Aren't Everything. I would say I will try, but no one can fall in love by trying."

"The Chattertree Woods is several days travel from the border," said Dr. Green. "So we have that much time to solve this riddle."

"Sounds good," said Dan. "I accept that I have to deal with Sister once and for all."

He would travel to Sister fast and use her truename before it changed. Maybe he couldn't love her. But he could kill her.

# HIDDEN THINGS

hey breakfasted by candlelight while the last owls hooted. "Our bacon and flour will keep a little longer," said Billy, "but here are the last Outland eggs." The creases in his face looked deeper than usual.

Dan was too worried to talk, but he tuned in when Alice said, "Excuse me, Dr. Green, but what name should we call you now? Are you still Dr. Green here?"

Dr. Green laughed. "That does sound out of place. Many will call me 'Prince,' but I want such formality from none of you and especially not from Dan; transference is tricky enough without the therapist, or former therapist, imposing that kind of status. I had an easy time coming up with my Outland name, because my fairy name translates as Greenjack. You can call me that, although I imagine it sounds weird to Outland American ears. So how about plain Green without the 'doctor'? Or just Jack?" He smiled. "All right with you, Dan?"

*Greenjack.* Weird. Really none of those options sounded

good, but it warmed Dan that his old therapist asked him in particular, and he said, "Sure. Fine."

As they swallowed their last bites, Crackerbones disappeared through the storeroom door and returned with arms full of gear that he dumped on the table, saying, "Best not to travel unarmed at any time. Especially bad to travel unarmed when your goal is to defeat Sister and whatever guards surround her." A gesture by Mother Ferny ignited lots more candles, and by the increased illumination they saw the table piled with weapons. "Dan already has bow and sword and knows how to use them," continued the goblin. "The rest of you Outlanders, take whatever you can handle. For you, Prince, please accept this." He handed Dr. Green—Greenjack?—a slender sword, much too long for a goblin.

Josh elbowed Dan and whispered, "Two words: Green. Jack."

It was true. Long ago, when Maggie learned she was a changeling, her appearance had shifted fairy-direction: emerald-ocean green eyes, floaty hair, and a general beauty buff. Being in Inland seemed to be doing something similar to Dan's former therapist. There still wasn't enough light to see his eyes, but his hair had changed from black with streaks of gray to silver with streaks of green, and his skin too was faintly tinted green. Thank goodness that hadn't happened with Maggie's skin. And thank goodness Green hadn't taken on the weird pointy facial features of the fairies; he still looked like his calm, sturdy self. Dan supposed he could get used to the changes. At least it would make it easier to think of him as Greenjack.

"Thank you, Crackerbones, for the fine gift," said...Greenjack. He stood to bow and accept the sword. "It is long since I practiced, but I hope muscle memory will serve."

"If your legend is true, your muscle memory alone will suffice against most opponents," said Crackerbones.

Josh had been in the college archery club with Dan, but he pushed aside a bow and said, "What my muscles remember wouldn't hit a barn door." He picked up a short sword, and Alice and Graciela selected long knives. The Gatekeepers had wanted Graciela to stay so that if Gatemoodle were attacked she could help defend it with the spiderwork magic she had learned during the last war. But Graciela was adamant that she join her friends in the quest to defeat Sister.

They belted on their sheathed weapons and shouldered backpacks heavy with food and waterskins—Greenjack was concerned that they might have to traverse a corner of the Crawling Desert. They walked outside as the eastern sky gave the first hint that day might actually come.

"Once again, Dan, we send you on a quest that is as dangerous as it is necessary," said Billy. "With your bravery and tenacity you have over and over proven our choice of you to be a good one. Though the path is hard to see and must be travelled speedily, this quest too we deem in your power." Then why did he look so sad?

"And this time you have the help of your three friends as well as the Prince," said Mother Ferny, trying to smile.

"Well, the Prince and Graciela anyway," said Crackerbones, giving a little shake of his head as he looked at Josh and Alice.

But Josh and Alice were staring at Greenjack. From one side of Dan, Josh whispered, "Two more words: Gan. Dalf."

From the other side, Alice whispered, "I hope he doesn't do a Gandalf."

"What are you talking about?" asked Graciela. "I saw the movie; Gandalf's a good guy."

"Yeah, the hobbits totally need his help, but—" began Dan, but Greenjack interrupted his whispered explanation.

"I will give Dan all the aid that is in my power," said Greenjack. "Farewell for now, Gatekeepers. I hope to return when we all have time to tell tales across a table filled with Billy's fine cooking.

"But now it is time to kintravel to Maggie. We will not reach her but will reach the border of the Marrowland nearest her. Dan, I know you have the ability. Am I right that the rest of you are unable to kintravel?"

Dan's friends nodded.

"No matter," said Greenjack. "I can easily carry three." But then he paused and furrowed his brow as he looked at Josh.

Josh sighed and said, "I know, I know, I'm too heavy."

Working at the Bagel Place, Josh had gained back some of the weight he'd lost running around Inland with Dan and Alice, but he still wasn't very heavy. Dan knew that wasn't the kind of weight in question. Billy Portman had once carried Josh and Graciela as he kintraveled, and Josh's "weight" had dragged them into the Shadowlands.

"There is no shame in being a true child of Outland," said Greenjack, "and I will gladly carry you and one other. Dan, can you carry one of the women? In need I could manage three, but that might force a detour through the Shadowlands, and although I am confident I could bring them out, even a short delay is to be avoided."

Josh shook his head vigorously. "No Shadowlands. Been there, done that, sucks big time."

"Sure, I can carry one," said Dan. He reached for Alice, but she took Josh's hand and they walked to stand beside Greenjack, giving Dan a look like, "We're a couple, remember?"

Dan wasn't sure why he hesitated a second before stepping over to Graciela. She noticed the pause, glowered, and said, "Yes, you take the booby prize." Dan told himself that her temper was the reason he'd hesitated, but that wasn't it. It was

42

the couple thing. Sister liked to play a mind trick that he was going to abandon Maggie for Graciela. That was stupid, Maggie was the most important thing in his life and he was never leaving her, but there was no denying that he and Graciela had felt electricity a couple times. That was in the past, but he had to be sure that even the memory of it wasn't a distraction, because to kintravel to Maggie his mind had to be filled with nothing but Maggie—distractions could land them in the Shadowlands.

"Sorry, Graci," he said. "You're no booby-prize. I'm just so worried about Maggie I don't know how I'm coming across. I'm going to close my eyes and concentrate. When I'm ready I'll hold out my hand for you. OK?"

"Sure."

"See you at the Marrowland," said Greenjack. He, Josh, and Alice vanished.

Dan closed his eyes. The simplicity of conjuring a full and deep vision of Maggie was a relief; after all, that's about all he had been doing during this time of worry. He held out his hand and felt Graciela's grasp.

As they swirled into the kintravel, a spark flew from her slender fingers into his.

When they landed, Graciela didn't let go. "Is this the Shadowlands?" she asked.

Dan was bent under the kintravel headache and exhaustion, and it took him a moment to open his eyes and look around.

"No, this is Inland," he said. But he squeezed Graciela's hand tighter. Greenjack, Josh, and Alice were nowhere to be seen.

DAN AND GRACIELA stood in a clearing bordered by thick vine-wrapped trees dripping grapefruit-sized blossoms of deep pink. The clearing was about thirty yards in diameter and perfectly circular in a way you never see in normal woods. Ankle-high grasses unblemished by weed or sapling covered the ground. The only sound was a susurrus of breeze that ruffled the grass but seemed not to touch the surrounding foliage. At the center of the clearing was a pool of violet water. Beside it was a large tent of the same color, with sides that almost imperceptibly swelled and sighed in the breeze. A path of clean white cobbles led from Dan's and Graciela's feet to the tent.

Dan noticed how tightly they gripped each other's hands and let go. He put his hand on his sword hilt and noticed Graciela rest hers on her knife. "Yeah, it doesn't quite feel safe," he said. "But, well, here we are. Shall we see if anybody's home?"

"What about going the other way, into the forest?"

Dan looked over his shoulder to where the cobbles entered the foliage. "That might be the Blossom Jungle, and Dr...I mean Greenjack or whatever, said it's dangerous."

"He also said the Blossom Jungle is in the Marrowland where you can't kintravel."

"Yeah, but I think rules maybe were broken. I lost concentration and the kintravel went wrong, because—well it doesn't matter why." But Graciela flexed the fingers that had been holding his and he knew she had felt the spark too. "Sorry I messed up."

"Never mind," said Graciela. "You should be the one to call a greeting. I feel like a man will be taken more seriously here."

Dan shrugged, cleared his throat, and called, "Greetings to whoever dwells in this clearing."

No answer.

Dan and Graciela walked closer and he called again, "Greetings. We come as friends. We request permission to enter."

Still no answer.

Dan drew his sword and Graciela her knife. They tiptoed to the entrance, nodded at each other, and flung aside the violet drapes.

Around the sides of the tent lay soft cushions of many colors. In the center was a king-size bed with a deep, inviting mattress. Over it was draped a gauzy canopy supported by bedposts carved with twining vines and nightingales. At the foot of the bed was a large hope chest of dark brown wood with floral carvings. On one side of the bed was a table laden with strawberries, apples, pomegranates, and fruits Dan didn't recognize, as well as pitchers of colored liquids. On the other side was a wooden stand holding a single book bound in leather of the same hue as the tent. The fabric walls were painted with scenes of leisure: men and women boating, men and women riding horses, men and women lounging on cushions. Always men and women, and many of the men naked to the waist, and many of the women too.

No one was home.

Graciela blushed. "We're intruding," she said. "I don't want to be in here when they come home."

"Agreed," said Dan. "That fruit looks good, but we have enough of our own food to last a while."

They backed out of the tent and looked around. Still no one to be seen. They picked a spot to sit in the soft grasses halfway between the tent and the jungle, where they could see anyone who came in by the trail and where anyone who came in could see them; they figured they would appear least threatening if they presented themselves openly, and there was nowhere to hide anyway. Well, nowhere except the jungle, and that option felt even riskier.

The fruit had looked really good. Dan poked around in his pack until he located the dried apples, offered them to Graciela, and gnawed one himself. "You know, I might be able to get us out of here," he said. "Not sure why I didn't think of it already."

"Kintravel again?" asked Graciela, gazing at the violet pool and the violet tent. She nodded. "That would be great!"

"Not kintravel. Like I said, I think we're in the Marrowland, but even if we aren't, I kintraveled to Josh once before, back in Mexico, and it got me close-ish, but I only actually found him because I knew the general area. Probably be better than that to just wait for Dr., you know, Greenjack to find us, like if you're lost in the woods you're supposed to wait for rescue instead of wandering farther and farther. But I can try Breaklock back to Gatemoodle. When I make a gate to Outland, it turns out the other side of the gate will go to somewhere I'm thinking of in Inland."

Graciela had gone back to staring at the tent. "Fancy magic! But maybe we should save that as a last resort. Greenjack might come looking for us here after we left, not know where we went. But...speaking of Breaklock, can I see it a sec?"

"How come? But, yeah, sure." Dan pulled the amulet out of his pack. Graciela touched it lightly, murmuring, "Yaxche's finger, Pacal's bracelet." Her father had originally created it out of a stick from that great ceiba tree, and the Mayan ruler's bauble. Dan looked at Graciela and shrugged.

"I'm not sure," she said. "It's like it wanted to tell me something."

Dan suddenly had the same feeling, but he didn't want to listen. He shoved Breaklock back in his pack and said, "Hey! Could you take us to our friends? You know, do your Grassy

Ella thing?" Grassy Ella was the name that seemed to fit the times that she did magic.

But Graciela shook her head. "I don't have power of my own. It's more like I'm a conduit. I've only been able to do magic in two places: the Natural History Museum when it was all charged up with power because Sister was there, and Gatemoodle, which is always full of power." The Natural History Museum episode was when they had lured Sister to Outland in hopes that she would lose her magic there. Hadn't really worked out, and Sister would have destroyed them except that Graciela was filled with a weird witchiness that enabled her to channel magical aid. At Gatemoodle, Graciela had guided spiders to make enormous nets to help defeat Sister's troops when they brought war.

Graciela was still staring at the tent, and Dan nodded. "Yeah, I'm curious too about who lives there."

And so they sat, nibbled dried apples, and stared at the tent until the sun went down. Dan vaguely wondered why he wasn't afraid something would come out of the woods. Luckily, when they laid back they discovered that the grasses were almost as soft as a mattress.

"I wish the others would find us," said Graciela.

"Me too. That's what Josh meant about Gandalf, by the way. He was super powerful and could help a lot, but he tended to go away for long periods of time and leave the hobbits to fend for themselves. Then he would reappear at some crucial moment. So far Greenjack is only the gone-away Gandalf."

\* \* \*

DAN OPENED his eyes to a sweet, unfamiliar birdcall. Graciela was already sitting up and yawning. She ran her fingers through her hair, picked up her glasses, and said, "I'm going to wash my face in that pool. Then let's check around inside again, see if we missed anything."

"Sure," said Dan. "Only, let's eat some of Billy's supplies before we go in. I don't want to be tempted by those fruits."

"Good idea."

Graciela had a weird expression on her face when she returned from the pool. "I guess it's OK," she said. "I sort of felt a twinge of…of I don't know. I guess it's OK."

Dan approached the pool slowly. The water looked cool and pleasant, and when he dipped his hand in it felt fine. Maybe because of the violet color it was strangely opaque, so he couldn't tell by looking if it was one inch deep or bottomless. He lay on his belly and stretched his arm in. If it had a bottom, he couldn't reach it. "I wonder…" he said.

"Wonder what?" asked Graciela.

"If Nellie Longarms could show up in this pool. Maybe that's what you felt. She always appears at the strangest times. We could use some help getting out of here."

"Do you think she can swim in the Marrowland?"

"Good question." Dan sighed. "Well whether she can or not, she's not here now."

Dan shrugged and turned with Graciela to the tent. He called out in case the owner had returned during the night. When there was no answer, they walked slowly up the path and eased the flap aside.

"No one home," said Dan.

"Someone was, though," said Graciela. "Look! The hope chest is open."

They walked closer, and Dan noticed something else. "Pretty sure that big book was closed before. Now it's open too."

Dan stepped up to the bookstand while Graciela investigated the hope chest. The book was open to an empty page. Dan tried to leaf through it, but in both directions the pages were stuck together. But, seemingly in response to his touch, letters began to form on the exposed page, at first too faint to read, then thicker and darker. The lettering was angular, almost runic.

"Hey," said Dan. He looked at the table of unblemished fruit, then back at the book. "It says, 'To escape, partake.'" The other pages came unstuck and he flipped through them, only to find the same message on each page.

"Mireme, Dan!"

Dan looked at Graciela. Weird that she had spoken Spanish, which he didn't understand. Weirder yet, she had changed her clothes for a gown of red silk with a border of golden pears— always-modest Graciela had taken a chance on being seen as she changed? The gown came to her ankles, but as she twirled and called out, "Que linda!" it swirled to mid-thigh. Tough Graciela acting all girly? Dan was about to protest when she reached into the hope chest and picked out a shirt for him, saying, "Una buen camisa para ti."

Dan reached for it. That shirt did look good. Comfortable and manly. Maybe seventeenth-century manly, or sixteenth or eighteenth—whatever, old fashioned. Dan slipped off his simple cotton shirt, hoping somewhere in the back of his mind that Graciela admired his muscles, and pulled the new one over his head. Some kind of material that was soft yet tough. The slit down the chest could be tightened or loosened with a supple leather thong. The shirt was all white except for the golden leather and small golden swords embroidered around the chest and the ends of the floppy sleeves.

Graciela was holding another garment toward him. "Pantalones," she said.

Trousers. Dan began unbuckling his old ones, then paused. "What did you call them?"

"Pantalones por supuesto."

Dan looked at what she held and smiled. Yup, those weren't pants: those ornate things deserved to be called pantaloons. He grinned. What a loony word: pantaloons. Then his grin left faster than it had come. He looked at Graciela. He looked at his shirt.

Loony.

"Grab your things, Graciela! C'mon, let's run outside!"

"What?"

Dan scooped up his old shirt and Graciela's old pants and blouse. He took her hand and tugged her toward the entrance. She resisted at first, but after they were outside she ran down the cobbles to the edge of the woods as fast as he.

"Give me those and turn away," said Graciela, blushing fiercely. Dan handed her outfit to her, turned, and changed back to his old shirt. In a moment he heard something crash in the branches. Graciela was back in her usual outfit, and she had hurled the gown into the trees. He pitched his fancy shirt in after it.

"So what did that book say?" asked Graciela.

"'To escape, partake.'"

"Those stupid clothes were supposed to make us partake of the fruit?"

"Yeah," answered Dan. "Yeah, except, maybe the clothes and the fruit were both..."

"What?"

Dan pictured the red gown swirling around Graciela's thighs. He remembered hoping Graciela liked his muscles and blushed. "Both supposed to make us do something else. Like Gawaine."

"What are you talking about? He was a Knight of the Round Table, right? I never liked that King Arthur stuff because it's unfair how Guinevere gets blamed for everything and all the women are basically seductresses."

"Yeah, that's the thing. I know about Gawaine because of my dad and his nutty Tolkien obsession. Tolkien translated an old story about Gawaine, and there's one part where a woman tries to divert him from his quest by seducing him."

Graciela had her arms crossed. "Typical."

"I think it's not just the fruit they want us to partake of," said Dan. "I think it's, uh, each other."

"'They, ha!" said Graciela, her face red again. "Sister set this trap."

"The good news is that Gawaine was able to resist."

Graciela didn't seem to be listening. Half to herself, she said, "And I was affected more than you. Does that mean...?" She frowned and looked at the ground.

"What's that?" cried Dan.

He was sure he had sensed something, but when he and Graciela whirled to search the woods, backing away, there was no one to be seen. Then a voice came faintly from the other direction, toward the center of the clearing: "Dan! Graciela!"

It was Greenjack's voice. He stood there with Josh and Alice, but while the morning sun shone brightly all around, they were dim as though illumined in pale moonlight. Greenjack frowned, looking back and forth between Dan and Graciela. Alice looked frightened. Josh was so dim that his expression could not be seen. All three began to fade, but when Josh had almost disappeared, Greenjack briefly shone clearer as though a cloud had passed from the moon's face. He pointed to Dan and then Graciela and called out, "Remember about hidden feelings, Dan!" Then they disappeared.

"What the hell was that?" asked Graciela. "Zoom psychotherapy, except no computer?"

"They must have been trying to kintravel to us," answered Dan slowly. "Josh is the one who's always hardest to kintravel, and he was the faintest. But this place has messed-up kintravel magic. We could get here, even though it's in the Marrowland, but they couldn't."

"It's a trap," said Graciela.

"Yeah. But I'm starting to feel like they'll get here. Greenjack is weird, but Dr. Green I trust. In fact, I feel like smiling for the first time since landing here, because that was a Dr. Green comment he made."

"OK, but meaning what? Maybe they will get here to rescue us, but it sounds like we have to do something too. 'Remember about hidden feelings'?"

"It's something that came up a lot in my therapy. Pretty basic idea I guess. It's the feelings that you aren't aware of that cause trouble. It's important to be open with yourself about how you feel, and a lot of times it's important to be open with others, even though it's embarrassing. But I don't know how that applies right now."

After a brief silence, Graciela said, "Isn't it obvious?"

"Not to me."

"Dan, we have to talk. There's black magic here trying to seduce us to sleep with each other, and the only way we'll be able to resist it is if we talk openly about our feelings for each other."

"What do you mean?"

"Stop that. We have to be truthful. I know you felt that spark when we held hands to kintravel."

Dan grimaced but nodded. "OK. I guess you're right."

The feeling of security from the day before was gone. Dan

and Graciela looked over their shoulders at the woods, and without a word hurried to the spot where they had spent the night. They sat and faced each other.

Graciela began. "Ever since Sister first saw us together, back when we lured her to my Natural History Museum, she's been making little knowing comments like you and I have something going on. Really every time she sees us. Am I right?"

Dan nodded.

"And there was that spark when we kintraveled, and we kissed that time in the Museum. Are you attracted to me?"

Dan leaned back a little but couldn't think of how to answer.

"C'mon, Dan. Dr. Green must have been telling us we're sitting ducks for our feelings to be manipulated by Sister or whoever owns that tent if we don't talk about them, get them into the open where we can see them."

"Uhh. Yeah, OK. OK. As far as kissing in the Museum, we agreed at the time it was just stress, and I still think it was stress. We'd just gone through that whole insane battle against Sister's evil creatures, helped by good creatures that were almost as weird, and you being Grassy Ella and all. So it was stress. But maybe not all stress. As far as the spark..." Dan trailed off. It would be just too stupid to bring up static electricity.

"I didn't actually ask you about the kiss and the spark. I asked if you're attracted to me."

Dan sighed. "Sure I am, Graciela. But don't tell Maggie. I don't even like thinking it just to myself, it makes me feel guilty. I have a girlfriend, and I love her and I'm going to marry her, and she's so gorgeous."

"Whereas I'm ugly?" snapped Graciela. "Skinny, brown, big nose?"

Dan sighed louder. "No, no, no, and no. I'm sorry I'm a

clumsy talker. OK, you want honesty. When I first met you I thought your looks…weren't for me. But then I got to know you, and—" Dan managed to make eye contact. "You're really pretty, OK? And smart. And strong, and good at getting done what needs to be done, I've been able to trust you since I first met you. Josh was turned on to you right away."

"You guys were talking about me?"

"Not in a bad way! Look, your turn, OK? How do you feel about me?"

It was a long time before Graciela answered. But just before Dan complained that it wasn't fair for her to ask him to talk and not talk herself, she said, "Ever since what Sister's Men from the Sea did to me, I've been turned off to boys, the whole hook-up thing. Hard enough to like myself with my mother dying, and Tía Josi getting crazy. Not to mention the creeps in college. But the Men from the Sea were the worst. And every time Sister insinuates you and I have something going on, it reminds me of the Men."

Dan knew about Tía Josi, how she had been a beloved mother-figure to Graciela after her real mother died, but then turned cold and hateful when Graci turned thirteen. Graci and her father had recently found out that she changed like that because Tía Josi's boyfriend Mr. Westerley—who happened to be Maggie's Outland father, divorced from her Outland mother —got tangled up with the King and Queen of the fairies in Inland. In hopes of curing Sister of her growing evil, the Queen had put on Mr. Westerley that stupid spell that whoever loved both his daughters would set them free, but then the King turned Mr. Westerley into a blue stag, and Tía Josi confusedly blamed Graciela.

And he knew that after Sister had turned the Men from the Sea prejudiced against "Big Noses" they had done—something

—to Graciela that made her hate Sister about as much as Dan did.

"Graci," he said, "I've tried to be a good friend and not ask you what the Men did because I thought you didn't want to talk about it. But maybe a better friend would have asked, so I'm asking now."

Graciela's lips were straight and tight, and her eyes glittered. "They groped me. All over. You'll say it could have been worse, my clothes stayed on, but those leering faces and those big dirty paws, it was awful, awful."

"I'm not going to say it could have been worse. It sounds horrible! I wish Josh and I could've rescued you sooner."

"But you did rescue me, and that's why it didn't get any worse. I don't think I've ever thanked you as much as you deserve. And working alongside you against Sister, and seeing how loyal you are to Maggie, and how much you love life here no matter how dangerous, and you try to treat everyone decently, even me—well, besides my father, you're the man who reminds me men can be OK. So if I let myself be interested in men, I'd let myself be interested in you. But you're with Maggie, and I'd never try to break up a couple."

Dan had a vision of a life where he'd never met Maggie, and he pursued his archeology interests when he got to college, and went to Mexico to study the Maya and met Graciela, and nothing was in the way of them getting together. Or maybe he went to New York City and bumped into Graciela in the museum and things started with an intense conversation about a dinosaur. Geeky ways to meet, but after all one of the cool things about Graciela was that she was into geeky stuff herself. But those gates were closed, and could never have been opened without closing the gate to Maggie and the Gates of Inland. He saw Graciela looking at him with a tear in her eye but a little smile, and he was sure she was thinking about gates too. They reached across the space between them and clasped hands.

When they let go, Dan realized that the sun was dipping into the western trees. "Let's build a fire tonight," he said. "And we should probably take turns sleeping so one of us can watch for danger."

They both gazed around at the forest. "I wonder if the woods is exuding this feeling of threat to scare us into the tent," said Graciela.

"I bet you're right," said Dan. "But even after our conversation, I'm not sure we're safe in there at night. Let's go inside tomorrow morning and see if there's some way to break the spell and get out of here."

"Agreed."

* * *

DAN'S NECK prickled as he splashed the placid violet waters on his face the next morning. He stood to scan the menacing circle of woods, and saw that no words were necessary; Graciela too was watching the trees. They nodded to each other and walked toward the tent. For the third time Dan called out a greeting, for the third time there was no response, and for the third time they pushed the flap aside to see no one at home.

"Kind of embarrassed to say this," said Dan, "but maybe those feelings we spoke about were making me jump to a wrong conclusion, you know, that this place wants us to partake of each other. Something about changing clothes felt funny like that, but maybe it just wants us to eat the fruit."

Graciela strode to the open hope chest and looked inside. "Think again," she said, as she pulled out a lacy, gauzy nightgown. "At least our conversation has made me immune." She wadded the nightgown and flung it back in the chest.

"And the book's turned black," said Dan. Once again runic letters formed when he touched the open page. "OK, this can't be good. It says,

'Third night comes.

My patience leaves.

Partake now

Or feel me weave.'"

With a rustle and whish, the tent flap closed and thongs wrapped around buttons to seal the opening.

"It doesn't even want us to wait till tonight," said Graciela. "Well, tough for it." She drew her knife and slashed the tent door, and she and Dan ran outside. Wind moaned through the blossom trees, and clouds scudding in front of the sun dulled the pink flowers to sullen red.

"Last resort time," said Dan, reaching for Breaklock. "I'm making a gate, and the backside should open to Gatemoodle. Run around there to check." Dan focused his mind on the big old table where he had shared many of Billy's meals, and performed the gate ritual. He hadn't focused on any place in Outland, but he knew the gate would aim for whatever location was closest to the front of his mind, and when he opened his eyes he frowned. The gate was flickering, and he could barely make out the comfortable chair in Dr. Green's office.

"No good!" cried Graciela from the other side of the gate. "It's just black here."

The wind moaned louder. "This way then, to Outland!" shouted Dan. But as Graciela ran to him the image faded to black, and the gate blinked out.

Dan grabbed Graciela's hand and said, "I'll try kintraveling to Josh." But whether because in his fear he couldn't properly concentrate, or because kintravel was indeed impossible in this spot, they remained rooted in place.

"Better to battle it here than in the woods," said Graciela. She drew her knife. Dan nodded and nocked an arrow to bowstring. They faced down the trail to where it disappeared among the trees. From the distance came a sound like boots on cobbles.

But a great roaring and splashing behind them drowned it out. Dan cursed himself for forgetting the violet pool. He turned as something monstrous emerged: body like a long-tailed fish, head like a slavering fanged boar, limbs that were somehow both fins and feet. It shook water from its bristly whiskers, only to cover them with drool, and fixed tiny red eyes on Dan.

"Ah, no! Una hoga!" cried Graciela.

Dan had no idea what una hoga was but he figured the only good one was a dead one. He loosed an arrow but the clumsy looking beast turned out to be incredibly agile. It sidestepped, twisted its neck, caught the arrow in its jaws, and crunched it so smithereens. Dan's second arrow bounced off its hide. Then the beast charged.

Dan and Graciela sprinted for the trees even though they heard footsteps loping toward them on the cobbles. Graciela held her knife forward—but lowered it with a laugh. It was Greenjack! He leaped from the trees as the hoga snapped its teeth inches from Dan's heels. Greenjack's sword flashed, the beast roared, and Dan turned, hoping to see death throes.

It wasn't going to be that easy. The hoga had dodged the blade and now it lashed its long tail at Greenjack who barely jumped aside. Greenjack spun and thrust but the creature reared and snapped and nearly caught the blade between its teeth. The tail lashed out again and again. Greenjack danced and circled so his back was to the pool and began moving toward it, dodging the tail, fending off snapping jaws with flicks of his blade, but slowly yielding ground.

"He's dead if he lets it chase him into the pool," muttered Graciela. "La hoga will be even faster there."

But Greenjack continued to retreat. When he was on the very verge of the water, the hoga roared and lunged straight at him. But its head butted nothing and its teeth snapped vainly because Greenjack had leaped high into the air. He came down with both hands on his sword hilt and all his weight behind it, and the sharp metal pierced the hoga from the back of its neck down through the throat. With another jump Greenjack pulled out his sword amid great gouts of violet blood. The hoga screamed and, clumsy now, lumbered into the pool. Waves splashed the shore, then ripples, and then the water lay still.

# BACK TO SCHOOL

*G*raciela's mouth hung open, and Dan realized his was doing the same. He snapped it shut as Graciela said, "I'm a whole lot more confident now about kicking Sister's butt, and her army too. Not to mention psychotherapy!"

Before Dan could reply, footsteps sounded on the cobbles behind. Just when he was starting to relax! He gripped his sword tighter and turned.

It was Josh and Alice, running out of the woods, their faces wrapped in garments that they now tore off. They gasped and walked in circles, hands on hips.

"Any trouble?" asked Greenjack, not even breathing hard. Josh and Alice shook their heads.

"One must not inhale the blossom perfumes," explained Greenjack. "Some are sweet and charming. Some are fatal. Some confuse the mind so the traveler wanders to a slower death."

"So you gave them a protective potion to breathe?" asked Dan.

"Only if you call my old sweaty tee shirt a protective potion," said Josh. "Hey! Alice...?"

"I know of no such potion for the Blossom Jungle," said Greenjack. "Fortunately, we were able to kintravel close enough that speed sufficed."

"But how will we get out of here?" asked Alice. "I don't know how much farther—"

"You guys should have seen it!" interrupted Dan. "Dr. Greenjack, that was incredible! I thought we were doomed and then you totally destroyed that—hoga, was it?"

Greenjack looked at Graciela. "I recall your father telling me its Mexican name." He smiled at Dan. "I encountered many dangers in my travels before my banishment. I am glad that my years of sitting in an office did not destroy my skills."

"I've wondered all along how we would deal with Sister's guards when we reached her," said Graciela.

"You guys should have seen it!" said Dan again. "I bet Dr. Greenjack can handle a whole army."

"*Doctor* Greenjack!'" Josh laughed. "I like it. Sounds like a new member of the Marvel Universe."

Greenjack laughed. "Armed guards may be the least of our problems. Billy told me that the Battle of Gatemoodle decimated her armies, and it will take time before she can assemble more than a scattering of goblins and other creatures. For her, as for me and all fairies, there is power in three." He winked at Dan. "Like in Outland fairy tales. So she will be guarded by a threefold task."

"What's a threefold task?" asked Alice.

"Wait! Look at the pool!" said Graciela.

At first Dan saw no change. It was just a pool. Then he realized that was the change: instead of violet, the pool showed natural blue with silver sparkles from the sun. Gradually silver overspread blue as though it was reflecting bright clouds, even under the cloudless sky. Near shore the water bulged as something pressed up from below. Dan readied his bow and looked to Greenjack for guidance, but the fairy prince did not reach for his weapon. He frowned, but not in a frightened way—was that sadness on his face?

Slowly, silver water sliding off and leaving them dry, three tall fairy knights rose from the pool and stepped ashore. From helms that hid their faces to sabatons they shone bright silver like the pool.

"We come for you, Prince," said the one in the middle—by voice a woman. "Your father's summons."

"How did you so rapidly locate me?" asked Greenjack.

"All the years of your banishment we have watched lest you return," answered the knight. "Only twice have the fireflies danced since we sensed you near the border. By chance we already were skirting the Blossom Woods and found this pool ready to hand." She gestured behind her. "It smells of Sally Wandil."

"You sense her too?" asked Dr. Greenjack. "It would greatly help our quest if you can tell us where she is."

"We do not know her place. She must dwell in the Marrowland to have created this scene, but we cannot feel her. She is masked by a threefold task."

One of the other guards looked at the tent, then at Dan and Graciela. "Twofold now," he said.

"Then that news is not all bad," said Dr. Green. "I with my companions must solve the tasks that remain and rescue the true daughter of the King and Queen. And better that you not hinder me—I am certain my father would support us in this deed."

"Support you he may, when he learns of it. We have not authority to make that choice. You must appear before him."

"Dr. Greenjack," whispered Dan, "they don't look as dangerous as an hoga. Can't we...?" He gestured a sword slash.

Out loud, Greenjack said, "Nay, Dan, I will not fight the Silver Guard. I am far from certain that I could hold my own, even with your help. But more than that, I will not shed the blood of my people unless in uttermost need, and dark as things are, they are not that dark. You and your friends have grown enough since I met you to rescue Maggie and defeat Sister."

"Two words," muttered Josh. "Gan. Dalf."

"But Dr. Greenjack," protested Dan, "can't you like magically instantly get to your father and explain what's going on and rejoin us?"

"No kintravel in the Marrowland, remember? We are in the far South. Even on the swift horses that I assume await the Silver Guard on the other side of this pool, journeying to the King will take seven days at least. Seven more to return."

"Too long, way too long," moaned Dan. "We've already left Maggie suffering way too long."

"It is time, Prince," said the central Silver Guard. The other two stepped on either side of Greenjack.

"But Dr. Greenjack, please answer my question first!" said Alice. "How do we get past the Blossom Woods?"

Greenjack turned to the central guard. "Grant me the duration of the skylark's flight song to seek the answer to her question within the tent."

The one he spoke to bowed, and the other guards stepped away. Greenjack strode into the tent. Dan wished he knew more about skylarks. For what seemed ages, the Silver Guard stood impassively, giving no clue. Just as Dan began hoping that skylarks sing all day, they turned and stepped toward the tent, hands on sword hilts.

Greenjack threw aside the door and walked toward Dan and his friends. Silver swords flew from silver sheaths.

"I need but time to tell them what I have learned," said Greenjack.

"Already we have delayed long enough to incur the King's wrath," said the guard.

Greenjack looked at Alice, and then at Dan. "If they do not learn what I have to tell, they will be in dire need." He placed his hand on his sword.

For a moment all stood frozen. Then, with the coordination of dolphins circling a baitfish school, the Silver Guard sheathed their swords and walked behind and to each side of Greenjack. The ones at his side gripped his elbows.

"Dan, Alice, Josh, and Graciela," said Greenjack. "My father compounds his foolish mistakes by thus interfering with my help, but I cannot prevent it. I believe he will regret this action, but it will be two weeks at least before I can explain to him and then seek you out, and that is two weeks too long. But as I said before, you have grown, and I deem you able to handle this final quest.

"To escape the Blossom Jungle you must partake of the fruit and drink inside. As Dan and Graciela know, it was imbued with romantic desire. The rage of the hoga has dissipated the local energy, and only mild desire remains, barely enough to coat the link to Sister herself. Partake of one, and you will travel beyond the Blossom Jungle in Sister's direction. Partake of two, you will find yourselves in the lap of the Chattertree Woods and Sister." The Guard began pulling Greenjack toward the pool. "Mild desire, as I said, yet still strong enough to feel."

Dan and Graciela edged apart.

"We got this," said Josh, holding Alice's hand.

"But wait!" shouted Dan. "Partake of one or two each, or all together? And—"

But Greenjack could only call out, "Farewell!" as the Silver Guard pulled him underwater with a faint splash. Dan ran to the edge and stared, but the surface remained opaque as the silver sheen turned blue.

"Normal color, at least that's good," muttered Dan. "But let's get inside and grab some fruit before some other weird thing shows up."

"Nice little love nest," said Josh when they entered the tent. "You sure we can't stay here a night or two?"

Alice nudged him. "Rescuing Maggie, remember?"

"So how do we do this?" asked Graciela. "How many do we want them to eat, and then like you asked, do they each eat that many, or eat that many in total?"

"The first question is easy," answered Dan. "We can't leave Maggie in truenamed torture a second longer than necessary. They eat two."

"We should each eat two," said Josh, smiling at Alice. "Because it's gonna be delicious, and since we don't have any other way to decide, at least we both get to enjoy ourselves."

"I don't know," said Dan. "If that counts as four... Damn! Why'd they have to take him away?"

"Dr. Greenjack said he trusted you to get this done, Dan," said Graciela.

Dan shook his head. "Us. He trusted us." He thought for a moment and then said, "We're all going to have a part in rescuing Maggie, I'm sure of it. But I'll go first. Here's how we do this: Josh and Alice each select two fruits but start out only eating one. If that only gets us part way, they eat the other. We want the romance to just affect Josh and Alice, so they hold hands while they eat. I'll hold onto Josh's shoulder, Graciela holds onto Alice."

Alice selected a peach and a pear. Josh said, "This stuff looks really good," and grabbed an apple and some grapes.

"Don't eat till we get outside away from the rest of it," said Dan. "I bet you're right it's delicious and I don't want you hogging down a bunch of them like at the old pizza place."

Halfway between the tent and the Blossom Jungle they took their stance.

Dan counted, "One, two, three, go." Josh crunched down on the apple, grunted, and took another savage bite. Alice smiled and licked pear juice from her lips. They locked eyes and kept eating. The world went dark, and Dan felt in his belly a sickly hollow that never came with kintravel.

* * *

LIGHT RETURNED.

"Minik Mingarria!"

Dan's shout echoed dully. He dropped Josh's shoulder and whirled, hand on sword, searching for Maggie, Sister, malkins... But what he saw was...

"A gym?" said Josh.

"An empty gym?" said Dan.

"Coach better not show," said Josh. "I hate gym class."

It looked like a full-size basketball court, with official hoops at the ends and a pair of practice hoops on each side. Basketballs lay scattered on the floor. Rows of bleachers awaited spectators.

"Two down," said Alice. "Strange hoga pool, Blossomtree Woods, one to go."

"And we're right in it," said Josh.

"I guess we should eat the other fruit," said Alice. Josh was already lifting grapes to his lips.

"No, wait!" shouted Dan. "We don't want to land right on top of Sister. Although something's very wrong about this place." He picked up the nearest basketball. "Not like I played a lot, but this doesn't look or feel quite right. The pebbling, or these lines around it?"

"Toss it here," said Graciela. She caught Dan's throw and made a layup off the nearest backboard.

"Nice shot!" said Alice.

"But too easy," replied Graciela. "The basket's a little bit low."

Josh still held the grapes near his lips. "Throw away the fruit!" said Dan. Graciela collected Josh's grapes and Alice's peach and then stood still, probably looking for a trash can. "This place feels like something Sister would make, so I agree we're in number three."

But his ring was still brown.

He strode to the door at the end of the gym and pushed the old metal bar to open it, then stepped back and let it slam shut. "Dark hallway, I don't like the looks of it. See if any of these doors open to the outside."

"At my Pomona gym it's the door in the middle, between the bleachers," said Alice. She tried it, and a beam of light came through the crack. The others crowded out behind her, glad to escape.

"Yes!" shouted Dan. The others stared at him; he stared at his ring and then held his hand up for them to see. "Remember my twining ring that's brown when I'm separated from Maggie, but turns greener as I get closer?" Actually, Dan's ring also turned green when he was near Sister. He never liked to think about that, especially because it reminded him of the stupid idea that he might love Sister too. "Now that I'm outside it's bright green. Although..." he frowned.

"OK, but why would Sister put Maggie in college?" asked Alice.

They all stared around, and then Josh said, "I'd hate to see the mascot."

The gymnasium behind them formed one side of a college quad. The buildings forming the left and right walls were made from weathered blocks of bare gray stone, like medieval halls; the building in front of them was constructed of new red brick peeking out of twining ivy with the big dull green leaves that come with age—ivy that should have been on the medieval walls, but they were bare. The grass was a perfect green, crossed with imperfect pathways, mixtures of paving stones, brick, and asphalt. No path led to an opening; the only way out would be through one of the building doors. One path petered out a few yards short of the not-quite-centered sculpture.

"I know that back in the normal world I'm supposed to appreciate big weird hunks of twisted metal as art," said Josh. "But that one...?"

Graciela wrinkled her nose. "It's like it smells bad, but there's no smell. More of a—"

"Let's get out of here," said Alice. "I don't see Maggie. Will your ring guide us to her?"

Dan was still frowning. "It's weird. Parts are bright green and other parts mostly still brown. Well, let's see if—"

"Wait, what's that sound?" asked Alice, pointing left.

They all cocked their heads. Faint and far away wafted a sound like dry leaves clattering in the wind, like children in daycare playing with rattles, like... "The Chattertree Woods!" shouted Dan. "Let's go!"

They took off running through the central lawn, Dan in

front, cutting across the grass, stumbling over misshapen paths, to the door at the middle of the building. Dan seized the heavy handle and yanked. And pushed and yanked again. It didn't budge.

"Of course it's locked," said Josh.

"Try the others!"

They ran to the doorway across from the gym, then to the last door, opposite to the rattle sound, but all were locked.

"OK, so back through the gym," said Josh. "You didn't like the dark hall, but I bet it leads out. How bad can it be?"

"Is that rattling getting louder?" asked Alice.

After a moment listening, Dan said, "No. It's the gym. Basketballs in the gym."

"OK, that's bad," said Josh.

"But it's the only door, if it's still open," said Dan, drawing his sword. "Everyone agree?"

They drew their knives and nodded.

Dan pushed open the door, and the dribbling pounded louder. The air smelled of sweat and disinfectant. They eased between the bleachers. Before Dan could take in the scene, someone bellowed, "Put the weapons away! Not allowed at college. Get in the game or get in the bleachers."

Dan hesitated—the voice sounded familiar.

"I mean now!"

Dan and his friends sheathed their weapons, vaulted into the bleachers, and clanked up the metal seats to the highest row, as far away as they could get, while the voice shouted, "Settle down! You disturb us."

They sat and watched two teams warming up. It was a little like that creepy croquet game that Alice got into in Wonderland. No flamingos, but everything was just wrong. The Skins team in front of them were kobolds, squat, hairy, with noses almost to their chins and carnivore fangs. Shirts were goblins. Each team had its own weird rules. Goblins were bouncing the balls to each other off the wall. Kobolds dribbled in circles until other kobolds tackled them. No one took practice shots.

"Win Fight Win!
Bite off their skin!
Blood on your chin
Now Win Fight Win!"

That was the kobold cheering squad. The goblin cheer-leaders countered,

"Butter their bread!
They're better off dead
First we'll score
Then off with their head!"

"Their eyes," whispered Graciela.

That was what bothered Dan the most. Every kobold that glanced toward them, every goblin that looked their way, had leaden gray eyes—not regular gray eyes, these were gray rim-to-rim, no whites at all.

A girl was crying on the bleachers at the other side. Maybe two girls, and it creeped Dan out. But no matter how hard he looked, he couldn't see them.

The biggest goblin faced away from them in the center of the gym, wearing a tunic with primitively painted referee stripes. He blew a whistle that sounded like a pig squeal and shouted, "Faster!" in that familiar voice. One of the kobolds put a basketball under his arm and wandered between the big goblin and the bleachers, then sat randomly at the edge of the court.

"I said faster!" The big goblin turned and cracked a whip at the kobold, who scampered back and crashed into a teammate.

The goblin glanced at Dan with his flat gray eyes, then turned back to the court.

The friends looked at Dan and he nodded. "Gragguts," he whispered. The leader of Sister's goblins, and he had seen Dan and all the others at one time or another, but he didn't seem to recognize them.

"Can we leave now?" asked Josh.

The door they needed was behind the kobold cheerleaders.

"Fight Win Fight!

We'll stab 'em tonight!

Pig knuckle, pig chuckle

Fight Win Fight!"

They sounded horrible, but the cheerleaders as well as all the players seemed to be off in some private mental zone, oblivious to the humans.

"Move quietly, and be ready to draw weapons," whispered Dan.

As they began their escape, the invisible girls wept louder. Dan halted and searched the bleachers again. Graciela nudged him and whispered, "Keep going. They aren't there."

But he had to know. He hopped down from the bleachers and ran to the other side, dodging kobolds. The weeping was louder now, but the weepers could not be seen. A kobold stumbled into him and snarled, "Yer girlfriend? Wish you'd shut her up. Maybe the prof knows where she is," and stumbled away. The weeping stopped like a switch was flipped. Dan stared around the gym but saw no professor, only his friends beckoning frantically. He wound his way back.

They tiptoed toward the door, but you can only be so quiet on old metal bleachers. When they reached the end and stepped down one row, it squeaked and groaned. Someone rifled a basketball that hit Josh so hard he started to topple, saved by

Alice grabbing his belt. Another ball zoomed straight at Dan and he snagged it just before it hit his head.

Mistake.

"That one's got skill!" shouted Gragguts. "Get him on the court!"

Kobolds swarmed up the bleachers and goblins ran from the other side of the court, shouting, "We get him! Our team!"

Dan beaned the closest kobold and drew his sword. His friends' blades whirred from their sheaths. The goblins and kobolds pulled up short. Dan and his friends jumped down from the bleachers, but the cheerleaders clustered together blocking the door. Goblins climbed over the bleachers and kobolds scurried underneath. Soon Dan and his friends stood back-to-back, blades out, surrounded by dead gray eyes and bared teeth. Dan looked over his shoulder at the door. Maybe they could kill a lot of them, but they would be swarmed over before they escaped.

Gragguts climbed to the top of the bleachers, waved a saw-edged scimitar, and blew his pig whistle. "Penalty!" he shouted. "Unsheathed weapons in the gym. Kill them!"

"Wait!" shouted Dan. "You have a weapon too! Same penalty on you!"

The pig squeal blew again, louder this time. "Double penalty!" screamed Gragguts. "Talking back to the gym teacher! Ten laps and a hundred push-ups each, after we kill you!"

Kobolds edged forward. Dan feinted with his blade and they fell back, but another pig squeal and they were on him, biting his ankles, yanking his hair. He heard Graciela and Josh cry out, heard tumult behind him.

Then they let go. Dan scrambled to his feet and saw Josh and Graciela lurch out of a pile of cheerleaders. All was quiet except the sound of a rattle. Alice was shaking Dr. Green's magic rattle, soothing goblins and kobolds with the rattle carved to sooth Maggie. The creatures smiled and blinked, eyes lightening from lead to tin. Dan and his friends backed toward the door as kobolds edged away from them. But Gragguts cocked his head to the side and furrowed his brow as he watched. It was as though the rattle was breaking some glamour, and Dan could almost see the light bulb go off over his head.

"I know them!" cried Gragguts. "The Golden Lady wants them, wants them, she wants them!"

Kobolds and goblins snarled softly and massed again in front of the door. Alice rattled louder, but it didn't help. Teeth gnashed, clawed fingers groped.

"Take my hand, Josh," called Alice. They locked fingers. Alice kept rattling, but now the timbre changed, brightened, the rattle sang like aspen leaves quivering together under a mountain sun. The kobolds and goblins sighed and smiled and moved away from the door.

All except Gragguts. He bounded down the bleachers, cracking his whip in his left hand, the scimitar in his right. Dan had seen Gragguts duel Crackerbones to a draw, and he knew Crackerbones was a way better swordsman than him or his friends. The whip caught Graciela by the ankle and pulled her down. Gragguts raised his scimitar and leaped.

"Catch!" shouted Alice. She threw the rattle at Gragguts, and dozens of kobolds and goblins swarmed for it, burying the big goblin. Dan and the others whirled, burst through the door, and sprinted down the dark hall. On either side as they passed, classroom doors were flung open and they heard students weeping while harsh voices shouted, "Who is disturbing our test?" They didn't look behind, even when they heard footsteps start after them, then fall back. When they reached the exit door they pushed as one and rolled out into the sunlight. Dan listened and heard no following footsteps or shouts. He slammed the door.

"Way to go, Alice!" shouted Josh.

"You were brilliant," said Graciela, rubbing her ankle where the whip had bitten.

Dan winked at Josh and Alice, and said, "You were great—I didn't even remember you still had the rattle."

"Too bad I threw it away at the end, though."

"But if you kept it we'd be dead," said Josh. "Hey, is that what's meant by a death rattle?"

Dan groaned and asked, "You OK, Graciela?"

She gave her ankle a last rub and straightened up. "I'm OK. But what in the world is this nightmare college all about? It's not my nightmare—I like college."

"Even gym?" protested Josh.

Graciela straightened her glasses. "I do a little intramural basketball."

"Let's figure this out later," said Dan. "Look! Listen!"

They were almost at the edge of the campus. The sidewalk passed between two buildings and then petered out on a grassy path that wound down a gentle hillside and passed into a broad woodland of odd-looking trees. A gust of wind bent the trees, and a moment later the rattling sound reached them. The forest stretched away into the blue distance, and Dan glanced at his ring. It was almost all green now, so they were headed the right way.

Dan hurried forward, the others just behind.

Above the door of the building on the left were the letters STEM. The door boomed open and a lumpy-looking professor lumbered out. At least, he was wearing professor-ish clothes: old running shoes, blue jeans, button-down shirt with loosely knotted tie, old sport coat. But his body almost burst the seams of his outfit, his hair was long and greasy, his eyes were beady, his skin was gray, and he was about ten feet tall.

"Leaving college already?" he grumbled, blocking the path.

"Well, I have a question first—Professor?" replied Dan. The troll nodded and drooled. "Who are those crying girls I couldn't see?"

The troll waved his hand in front of his face and grunted. "Those two mixed-up girls. We love 'em but we hate 'em. No more questions! Back to class!"

"Uhh. We never even enrolled here at all," answered Dan. "I mean, we go to other colleges. We're just visiting."

The troll professor frowned. "There is no other college to equal Troll College. How do you expect to get a job if you leave without completing your degree?"

"Uhh. It's summer vacation anyway."

"Summer term is one of the best times to study. Other students gone, fewer distractions. I must insist that you go back into the quad. Classes are already in session. If you haven't registered yet you can audit today and take care of the paper-work tomorrow."

"OK, great, awesome, we're leaving now," said Dan.

"Haw!" said the troll professor. "You may leave if you answer a graduation question. Otherwise, I will kill you all!"

"Wait, what happened to the going-back-to-class option?" muttered Josh. Alice elbowed him, and he said, "True, this guy killing us is probably better than class."

"Guys, look at him," said Dan. "We can outrun him. On the count of three: One, two—"

"Haw, haw!" laughed the troll. "Most of you might get away, but I will catch one. Will you leave a friend for my stew pot? An arm today, a leg tomorrow? Haw!"

Dan sighed. "What's the graduation question?"

"I'll make it an easy one," said the troll. "What is the cosine of the cantilevered quark?"

Dan looked at Graciela, then back at the troll. "Uh, I know some archeology," he said.

"Haw, haw, haw. Archeology is not a science. It is practically history."

"Maybe not, maybe so," said Graciela, "but this examination is totally unfair. All of us are more Humanities types."

The door of the other building creaked open and out walked the female version of the thing in front of them. She had a tote bag over her shoulder, two big volumes clasped to her chest, and thick round glasses. She also had green skin, and six-inch tusks sticking up from her lower jaw, and she was just a tall as the male.

"Well, well," said the first troll. "Here comes the chair of our Humanities Department, and just in time. Give us a graduation question, Professor!"

She shoved her books into her tote bag and scratched her chin. "They look kinda dumb, so I'll make it an easy one—but wait!" She furrowed her brow at Graciela. "This one has a question."

"Yes, ma'am," said Graciela. "Umm, I've been stuck on it but I had no idea you're the one to ask."

"Stop wasting my time!" roared the troll. "Ask!"

"What do I need to know about the bracelet and the stick?"

"Stupid question, how should I know?" But then the troll slapped her head like a gnat had bitten her, and mumbled, "Not given forever. Always you take from your fathers, now what you've taken it's time to give back."

"Graduation question!" roared the other troll.

"Yes, yes, here it is: In the fifth canto of Paradise Lost, what did Hamlet say to Autolycus, and why does syndecdoche?"

Dan had strung his bow by then. "Sorry, Professor," he said and sent an arrow whistling to the first troll's heart.

It bounced to the ground. "Haw, haw, hee!" laughed the troll. "The Golden Lady thickened our skin."

"Run!" shouted Dan.

He and Graciela broke left, Josh and Alice right. The trolls were smarter than they looked, and faster too. They ignored Josh and Alice, backhanded Graciela, and had Dan gripped in their huge mitts almost before he knew it.

"Make a wish," said the female troll to the other. "You pull his right arm, I'll pull his left, whoever gets the bigger piece eats it all." Dan felt his joints creak.

"Eat this if you're so hungry!" said Graciela. She held out the magic fruit she had confiscated from Josh and Alice.

The pressure on Dan's shoulders relaxed a little. "We are professors, remember?" said the male troll. "We are not dumb. How do we know it is not poison?"

Graciela popped a grape in her mouth, chewed, and swallowed.

The trolls took the rest of the fruits in their free hands and shoved it in their mouths. They dropped Dan, hugged each other tightly, and plastered their faces together.

Then they pulled away and the male said, "Your place or mine?"

"Mine is warmer."

Hand in hand, they lumbered into the Humanities building.

Dan rolled his shoulders to make sure they were OK. "Thanks, Graciela, wow, your turn to be brilliant, you saved me. And that was brave, you could have fallen in love with them, yuck. I guess one grape wasn't enough."

Josh and Alice were tugging at them. "Let's go, let's go," urged Alice.

"You guys go on," said Graciela. "I really do love college, and the Humanities prof was smart." She turned and started back toward the classrooms.

"Oh no you don't!" said Dan. He and Josh got in front of her, and Alice put her arm over her shoulder. "Graci, we're going to get you back to Columbia," said Dan. "In the meantime, I don't think you ever told Josh and Alice about your research, and I bet they'd love to hear about it."

"Probably nothing I'd rather hear more, that's a great idea," added Josh.

"And great ideas are what I love about college," said Graciela, as Alice steered her toward the Chattertree Woods. "So here's what I'm working on…"

# CHATTERTREE WOODS

"What's our plan?" asked Josh.

"Follow my ring," answered Dan, waving his hand in the air. The color could barely be seen in the dusk, but he knew it was mostly green. "Carefully. We may have to fight malkins or goblins or something, so have weapons ready. And I'll be ready to shout Sister's truename as soon as I see her."

"What about what the Gatekeepers said, that her truename maybe has changed?" said Alice.

"But no good trying in the dark," said Dan, ignoring her. "We'll wait till morning."

They had found a nook that sheltered them from the breeze, in the side of a little hill far enough from the road that wandering trolls or other creatures wouldn't bump into them. A lone Chattertree, like an advance scout from the woods, leaned over them. Its pods looked like the long-necked gourds that Dan and his family used to use as Thanksgiving decorations, but old and dry like a long-overlooked centerpiece.

"Does anybody have any idea why Sister created a college to intercept us?" asked Graciela, passing out bread and cheese from her pack. Billy had done something to help it maintain freshness, but it wouldn't last much longer. "I have a thought, but it doesn't seem likely."

"I've been thinking she took it from my mind as something scary," said Josh. "I'm not really into college. 'Indifferent' would be the college word for me. But yeah, how will I get a job better than the bagel place if I don't graduate? STEM, ugh. But they make the money. I'd try that if I had the brains."

"Stop pretending you're dumb, Josh," said Alice. "And why would Sister take something from your mind that didn't fit the rest of us? I like college."

"I like it a lot," said Graciela, glancing back toward Troll College. "I'm glad I only ate one grape."

"Me too," said Josh with a wink. Graciela had kept haranguing them about her research until finally winding down just a minute ago.

"I used to worry there might be no job I'd like, even with a degree," said Dan. "But that's not important now that I've found Inland." Then a deep hollow opened in his stomach. What if he failed to save Maggie, failed to save Inland, was exiled back to the regular world? Quickly he continued, "But even if we all hated college that was a stupid way to try to stop us. All those goblins, kobolds, and trolls would have caught or killed us easy if they hadn't been stupefied into playing college roles. It's like the ones in the gym were enchanted to overlook us."

"Here's what I think," said Graciela. "Someone interfered with Sister's magic."

"Some powerful magician we don't know about is on our side?" said Josh. "That would be awesome!"

Dan shook his head. "I don't think so. Anybody with power

like that, Billy or Dr. Greenjack or the Silver Guard would have been aware of them and told us."

"But that just leaves Maggie or Mrs. Westerley," said Alice. "Even if Mrs. W's gotten nicer I can't believe she'd help defeat her daughter, and from what you've described about truenaming, Maggie's a helpless slave—sorry."

"You know, Dan, don't you?" said Graciela.

It was almost completely dark now, but Dan sensed them all looking at him. He sighed and said, "It's Maggie. They've had a connection all along. Maybe that's why I'm supposed to love them both, though I still don't get that. When Mother Ferny made my ring so it would guide me to Maggie, it ended up reacting to Sister too. And I noticed today that the green parts are brighter than ever—it senses Maggie and Sister together now. The two invisible crying girls in the gym? Maggie and Sister, mixed-up like the troll said. Sister's always wanted to capture Maggie, always talked about how strong they'd be together. And Billy learned from their gate that she's forcing Maggie to merge with her, to feed her power with Maggie's."

"If she's doing that to get more powerful, why'd she come up with weak-ass Troll College?" asked Josh.

Dan puzzled over that for a moment before answering. "Sister's mind must be mixed-up by Maggie's. Maggie knows we're all in college, so if she's hoping we'll rescue her that might put college in her mind."

"That explanation?" said Josh. "Two words: Weak. Ass."

Alice elbowed Josh and said, "Because Maggie has no idea any of us but you would be here."

"And if the main thing she thinks about you is you're in college, I feel sorry for both of you," said Josh, guffawing. "And what was all that about you having a question, Graciela?"

"It's about Breaklock. It kind of called to me when Dan and I were stuck in that place you found us. And believe it or not the troll wasn't quite as dumb as she looked, because her answer about my father helped me figure it out. Just a reminder that Breaklock is on loan."

Dan nodded slowly. "I felt it too. Yeah, I'm supposed to return it if I finish my quests—free FCB, free Maggie. And that's OK, because if I do that the Gates of Inland will be open enough for me to go back and forth without Breaklock."

Alice said, "No 'if,' Dan. Sister hasn't mastered Maggie yet. We have time!"

"Only a little," said Dan.

"And we must be close," said Alice. "Strange hoga clearing. Blossomtree Woods. Troll College—we've completed the three-fold task!"

* * *

DAN LAY THERE but couldn't sleep. The moon rose late and was only a little more than half full. He had to reach Maggie soon not only to rescue her from torment but so they could get married in time. He had been given three months, and almost a week of the second month was gone.

He heard Josh creep toward him from the spot where he had bedded down with Alice.

"Dan, good buddy?"

"Yeah?" whispered Dan.

"I'm scared. Don't tell Alice."

"I'm scared too." Somehow Josh's comment warmed Dan, and he smiled. "Don't tell anyone."

"I don't think it's going to work just going around bellowing Minik Mingarria," said Josh. "You'll have to have something else. I like to tease you about loving Sister, but I agree that's impossible."

"Then what?" asked Dan.

"Once she masters Maggie's power, won't her truename change?"

"Thats all I've been thinking while I stare at the moon."

"What will it be?"

After a pause, Dan said, "I'm working on it."

Josh clapped him on the shoulder. "Then I'm not scared any more. You da man." But Dan knew it wasn't just the need to whisper that made his voice small.

* * *

DAN HAD the fire going and a pot of water hot before the stars faded. The others—even Josh—woke soon after and made coffee with the last of Billy's Outland grind. Dan dumped his after one sip; he was already too wired with anticipation. After a few bites of trail mix they packed silently and followed the path to the edge of the woods. The pods hung quietly in the still air. Dan felt everyone looking at him. He nodded, said, "This is it," lifted his ring into view, and stepped among the trees.

His ring flashed solid green.

"Minik Mingarria!" Was it green for Sister? Or for Maggie? But neither was there. Nothing happened except that the pods began to rustle.

"Your ring, Dan!" cried Alice.

His ring pulsed bright green, faded to brown, and then turned black as a moonless, starless night.

"Her truename killed it," groaned Dan.

Everyone had seen it; there was no need to say anything

else. Behind them was a clear path back to Troll College. No good. All around them were Chattertrees, rattling louder now. The foliage was open enough to let light in even from the low dawn sun, and the undergrowth was short except for occasional patches of bracken, so walking would be easy, but it was a uniform landscape where they would just wander uselessly.

"I thought we'd completed the threefold task," said Dan. "Finding Sister should be easy now."

Suddenly, where before them had been random woodland, a path appeared. It ran straight ahead, a dirt rut bordered by grass dotted with strange white flowers.

"There!" said Alice. "Easy."

"Maybe too easy?" said Dan. He nocked an arrow loosely to his bowstring and started forward. If Maggie had been with him, and Sister just a memory, it would have been pleasant. As they got farther in, some of the trees grew bigger, with larger pods that rattled more deeply, and the mixture of tones ebbed and flowed soothingly with the changeable breeze. Dan could see how Mrs. Westerley would like it. The white flowers winked in the sun, and where they bloomed most thickly butterflies puffed up around their knees. Unfamiliar birds fluted from either side. A pair of black vultures like Piebald with big white ruffs floated high above them and then angled away, but Dan sensed no malevolence. Just ordinary vultures searching for carrion.

But Maggie wasn't with him, and Sister was more than just a memory. His ring stayed black. Dan knew from the shortening shadows when noon arrived, and he heard Josh speculating about when they would stop for lunch, but he merely pulled trail mix from his pack and munched while walking. After a while, Josh's sighs behind him were followed by sounds of rustling and chewing.

84

All the while, as their shadows grew longer before them, the path continued with no hesitations or forks. It seemed to be straight, but Dan knew that among these uniform trees he couldn't really tell whether it was curving or even slowly returning them to where they started. And it could be a path leading to some stupid place that had nothing to do with Sister. Dan tried to shake those thoughts out of his brain. They could go back, which would be giving up, or leave the path, which would be getting lost, or continue.

Another instrument joined the pods and birds, plinking and swishing. It grew louder and they came to a swift dark creek flowing through a clearing. Some jumbled rocks made for a dry crossing, and Dan saw the path continue on the far side. He threw down his pack.

"Hey, Davy Crockett, why are we stopping?" asked Josh. "I mean, I'm not complaining, but even I can tell there's a couple hours of daylight left."

"This is probably the right path, but what if it's not?" said Dan. "Maybe Nellie Longarms is in this creek, and she can help us."

Josh and Alice, who had been standing at the edge of the creek looking in, backed away.

"Help us how, Dan?" asked Alice.

"I don't know. I don't pretend to understand Nellie. But every trip to Inland she's helped Maggie and me. Sometimes by killing enemies with those long arms and fangs. Sometimes by magically transporting us underwater. Sometimes just with information. I don't know how she and I became...friends...in this special way."

"She's special all right," said Josh. "Did you bring tuna?"

"No."

Josh backed even farther from the creek. "Then she'll probably use those long arms and fangs to catch and eat one of us."

"I wish I had brought tuna, just as a present," said Dan. "But she's released me from the promise to always bring her Outland food."

"Dan saved her life," said Graciela. "Brought her back to life, really, with the Makeless Made spell. It's to pay for that spell that he has to leave Inland if he and Maggie don't marry. She was helping us in the war at Gatemoodle, and Noggles suffocated her by keeping her on dry land, and Dan saved her. You guys stayed in Outland that time, but I saw it. I don't think we need to worry about Nellie."

"OK, what about Noggles then?" asked Alice, squinting at the water. "Another deadly water creature, and they're never good."

"We're nowhere near an ocean, and Noggles prefer salt water," said Dan. "We'll camp here tonight, give Nellie that much of a chance to appear."

* * *

As the first stars twinkled into the clearing, Graciela joined Dan where he sat on a big rock in the middle of the creek, staring into the water. "Do you think she'll come, Dan?" she asked.

Dan shrugged and sighed.

"Is your ring still black?"

Dan nodded.

"Josh had an idea, but he didn't want to come near the water, but I don't mind," said Graciela. "He wondered if maybe your ring's not actually dead. Maybe it just hates Sister's truename, but Maggie's could bring it back to life."

"I guess it's worth trying," said Dan.

"I'll go back on the lawn; I don't want to hear her truename," said Graciela.

"It's OK, I'll whisper." Dan put his lips by his ring and breathed, "Maggie Magpie."

His ring pulsed green and then returned to black.

"What does that mean?" asked Graciela.

"Not dead, but not any use either. Sister must have a spell on these woods to keep it from working here. I guess that tells us she's in these woods, but we knew that anyway."

* * *

DAN POPPED AWAKE, not sure if the splash he had heard was in a dream or real. The waning gibbous moon illuminated his sleeping friends. Josh snored, muttered, and rolled over, and all was silent.

There! That was a real splash from the creek. Dan rolled out of his blanket, padded across the lawn, and stood shivering on the rock midstream. Small insects popped out of the water and fluttered near the surface. "Nellie?" Dan called quietly. "Nellie, is that you?"

But when the splash came again it was only a large trout, surfacing to suck in one of the insects. Dan watched a while longer, just in case—and because of the way the pinks and blues on the flanks of the trout had glowed in the moonlight. Other fish joined the feast, but no Nellie. He turned back to camp when a sheet of clouds was pulled over the moon. First the pool by the tent—an hoga came out of that, not Nellie—and now this creek. There was no relying on Nellie Longarms.

A wet hand clamped his ankle! Dan smiled and looked over his shoulder—but in place of Nellie's beautiful cat face he beheld the algae-thatched fangs of Jenny Greenteeth. His shout of terror was stifled by her other hand as she yanked him into the creek.

Jenny leered close and he felt her marshy breath on his face, but just when he was sure time was up, she shifted her mouth to his ear and whispered. "Will you stay silent lest you alert the witch to me, cousin-friend?"

Dan nodded, and Jenny released him.

"I am allowed few words and those quiet, or the witch will hear," she said. Unseen in the darkness the leaves overhead began to rustle. Jenny's eyes flicked up and then back to Dan's face. "She knows Nellie is your friend, she has blocked Nellie from her woods, but not Jenny, not yet." From somewhere on her person she produced a small box. "Water cousins made these to protect you from your truename."

Dan opened the box and saw what looked like two blobs of seaweed. "Earplugs! To block her voice," he said.

"Cannot block truename. Change so only waves you will hear. They will work only on the witch's voice. And they will hurt so use only when you must."

The leaves rattled. "I must go. But this message Nellie sends: 'Time of the long swim grows near.'"

"What does that even mean?" asked Dan. But the wind gusted hard and Jenny dove beneath the water and was gone.

Dan stumbled back to camp. As he rolled himself into his blanket, Josh muttered, "A horse."

"What? Where?" said Dan.

Josh snored and murmured, but the only words Dan could make out were, "Funny horse."

* * *

PERHAPS BECAUSE OF his nighttime awakening, Dan wasn't the first one up in the morning. But Alice's voice got him up fast.

"Where are we?" she wailed.

It took a moment for it to register on Dan. They were in the clearing, the creek chuckled nearby, rocks crossed the middle of it, and Chattertrees rattled gently all around—all fine.

Except the trail was gone.

Dan looked where they had come from, pulled on his clothes and crossed the creek to study the far side of the clearing, and then walked slowly back. "No sign of a trail in either direction," he said. "I don't think the Blossomtree Woods counted. Greenjack told us that forest is a regular part of the Marrowland, so it's not something Sister crafted. We're still on task three."

"You can figure our direction anyway, right?" asked Josh. "Moss on the whichever side it is of trees, or by the sun—does that work when it's cloudy?"

"There's no moss on any side of these trees," said Dan. "It's too dry. We can sort of tell where the sun is even with the clouds, so we'll try that. Trouble is, the canopy's a lot thicker across the creek, and that's the direction we need to go."

Josh walked up and down the creek while the others got food out. When he returned, Dan raised his eyebrows.

Josh smiled lopsidedly. "Looking for hoofprints. I thought I saw a horse last night. We could ride out of here."

"You were dreaming," said Dan. "You talked about it in your sleep. You said it was funny—what was so funny?"

"Well. Not haha—ah, never mind, it was just a stupid dream. But no stupider than you hoping for Nellie Longarms, I guess."

"Actually…" Dan told them about Jenny Greenteeth and her gift.

"Excellent! We are getting somewhere!" said Graciela. "And I don't know that we can completely discount dreams here. The trail just disappeared, and I say that's stranger than dreaming. Sister is strong."

"Well if anyone does see a horse, tell the rest of us and stay close," said Dan. "There were tatterfoals around Gatemoodle last time, and they try to lure you onto their backs and carry you away."

Behind them came a burst of rattling as a falling pod struck the ground, and they all jumped.

"Let's go," said Alice. "I don't like this clearing and creek anymore."

IT WAS AS DAN FEARED. After they trooped across the creek and into the trees on the other side, the woods changed. There was no more grass, of course, or butterflies, and they crunched over dry leaves and pods, circling around patches of brambles or waist-high bracken. The trees grew taller and thicker, their pods larger and more numerous. Occasional pods fell to the ground, and the rattling was no longer soothing but ominous. At first, Dan got glimpses of the cloudy sky through openings in the canopy and was able to make a good guess at their direction, but the openings grew fewer, and smaller, and finally disappeared altogether. Dan pretended he still knew where they were headed, because he didn't want to stop and didn't want to scare everyone, but for all he knew they had veered off in a completely different direction or gone in a circle. Eventually he called lunchtime, looking up at the sky and pretending to tell the time that way, but really he based it on Josh's grumbling.

"I don't think you fooled them," whispered Graciela,

nodding her head toward the big tree that Josh and Alice had chosen to lean against. They were frowning and whispering too. "Is your ring still black?"

Dan held up his hand so she could see: still black.

"I've been thinking," said Graciela. "Maybe it means something that it flashes when you say their truenames. Maybe it's trying to tell you something that will help us find our way."

"We need something to go our way," said Dan. "I'll try again. Minik Mingarria."

Pulse to green, return to black.

"Now Maggie's," said Dan, leaning toward his hand to whisper.

Graciela put her hand over the ring and said, "Wait. It's so quiet in here I'm afraid I'll hear even a whisper. Wait till I'm over there with Josh and Alice."

Dan watched her walk to the others and join their conversation, then whispered, "Maggie Magpie."

Pulse to green, return to black. But was it different this time? Dan thought it had pulsed a little longer, a little brighter. "Maggie Magpie," he whispered again, and then "Minik Mingarria." Crap. There was no difference. He caught Graciela's eye and shook his head.

"Hey!" Josh's shout cut the gloom. "Hey, hey, hey!" Josh was up and running. "Horse!"

"Josh, stop!" shouted Alice and Graciela, crashing right behind him. "Could be a tatterfoal!"

By the time Dan caught up with them, Alice was holding Josh by his belt, and Graciela stood in front with her arms spread, blocking him.

"So where's the horse?" asked Dan.

"It was right over there," said Josh, gesturing vaguely in front of them. "I might still see it if these guys hadn't stopped me."

"Tatterfoals really are bad news," said Dan. "One of them almost got Maggie and me, so stop charging after it."

They all scanned the woods. Finally Graciela said, "These tree trunks are basically horse color anyway. Be hard to see it even if it was right by us."

"Uh-uh," said Josh. "That's what was funny that I didn't want to say before because you'd laugh at me. This horse is blue."

"Guys," said Alice. "Where are our packs?"

Dan groaned. They had run out of sight of their packs, and the woods looked exactly the same in every direction.

Sticks cracked in the near distance. They all looked at each other. Another stick snapped.

"I say it's my horse," said Josh.

"And I say it's something at our packs," said Dan. "Let's go."

More slowly this time, they headed toward the sound. Alice and Josh breathed sighs of relief when their packs came in sight. Graciela motioned them to wait, and Dan crept forward, arrow nocked.

"I think it's OK," he called. "Our stuff looks fine, and no one is here."

"Any hoofprints?" asked Josh.

Dan scanned the ground. "It does look scuffed up over here, but I can't make out any prints. Josh, did your horse have antlers?"

"Horses don't have antlers," said Josh. "Duh."

"Because there's a giant blue stag that has helped Maggie and me more than once."

"And he's Maggie's father," said Graciela.

"Oh, wait. No no no no no!" said Josh. "Maggie's father is a Fairy King who sometimes is a skeleton. That's bad enough, don't you dare tell me her father is a deer! Dan told us that nonsense back when he showed up at my house to bring us here, but I ignored him. Now you, Graciela?"

"Yeah, I meant adoptive father," said Graciela. "The King of the Fairies, Maggie's birth father, cursed the mortal father and turned him into a big blue deer. He was crucial in the war at Gatemoodle. He crushed the malkins, and when Sister was about to use the unlight he knocked it out of her hand and crushed that too, even though her red ravens almost killed him."

"Maggie begged the King of the Fairies to change him back into a human then," said Dan, "but he wanted to stay a deer. I think because he's in love now in Inland. He was helped back to the woods by a beautiful white doe.

"So if your blue horse, which makes no sense in the woods or really anywhere, is a blue deer, we should follow him."

"And there he is!" said Josh, pointing.

Dan saw something blue flit past distant trees, gone after a glimpse. He marked the spot in his memory and said, "Grab your stuff. Let's go."

"But Dan, if he's really your helper and not one of your tatterfoals or something worse, why doesn't he show himself clearly?" asked Alice.

"Good question, and I don't know the answer," said Dan. "But I do know that it's no good staying here and starving or waiting for goblins to find us."

He shouldered his bag and led them to where they had seen whatever it was. When he reached the spot he halted, hands on hips, and looked around. Nothing. A pod crashed to the ground and he whirled. Nothing.

"There!" said Josh.

Dan looked where he was pointing but saw nothing.

"I see it!" said Alice.

This time they all saw it, and hurried to the spot, and stopped, and looked.

The whole day went like that. When it was almost too dark to see deer or horses of any color, Alice said she saw its head, and it didn't have any antlers. Hot, dusty, and discouraged, they threw down their packs and put supper together.

As they pulled out their blankets, Alice said, "That means it's not your deer, right Dan? No antlers? So it's a bad tatter-thing?"

"Even in Inland the stags must lose their antlers and grow new ones every year," said Dan. "So I haven't given up hope. I don't know why it doesn't show clearly if it wants to help. On the other hand, I don't know why it hasn't attacked if it wants to hurt us. We'd better keep a watch tonight. I'll go first."

No one saw anything that night, or heard anything other than the rattling, and an occasional pod clunking on the ground. The next day Graciela sighted the blue creature first, and the morning proceeded much like the day before. Only the frisson of hope against fear kept monotony away. After a while Dan noticed the trees begin to grow less thickly, and eventually patches of sky showed through. The clouds were thicker than ever though, so he still couldn't see the sun to judge time or direction. Not that he had a clue what direction to choose if he could judge it. Thunder grumbled far away.

Suddenly they stumbled into a clearing maybe twenty yards across, and there on the far side, plain as day, stood the big blue animal.

"That's no horse," said Josh, "even if it doesn't have horns."

"Antlers," said Dan, and burst out laughing. "But horns, antlers, who cares! We're safe."

The dust puffed up beside the deer. It snorted and looked into the branches at the side of the clearing, halfway between it and Dan. It danced to the side, and dust puffed up from where it had been standing.

"Someone's shooting darts at it!" said Dan.

"Why doesn't it run?" asked Graciela.

Dan had an arrow nocked but he couldn't spot the shooter among the branches. He saw a small arrow flash out, and guessed and shot his own arrow, but heard it whish harmlessly through leaves. Another dart flashed out, and this one pierced the blue deer's haunch. Finally it limped into the trees. Leaves shook as whatever was in the branches pursued it. Dan nocked another arrow and started after it.

"Stop, Dan! Look!" called Graciela.

Dan kept running but glanced over his shoulder, and then he did stop.

A white doe stepped into the other side of the clearing, seeming to glow even under the leaden sky. She nodded at Dan and then stepped back into the trees. Dan took a step toward her but then turned back toward where the blue deer had disappeared.

"I think he'll be all right, Dan," said Graciela. "The blue deer is smart. He can take care of himself."

Dan nodded and placed his arrow back in its quiver.

They saw her again as soon as they left the clearing. "She's beautiful," sighed Alice. "I feel better just seeing her."

The white doe stayed just in sight, flitting in and out of the trees as they followed. Dan thought about Alice's comment. Sister was beautiful when she wasn't looking mean. Mother Ferny was a warty-nosed witch but was as good as could be. Beauty wasn't much of a guide, in Inland or probably Outland either. No matter. This doe was the mate of the blue deer, and they had proven their good hearts already.

"I think I know what was going on," he said. "The blue deer was trying to guide us but had to keep disappearing to avoid whatever was hunting him. Now he's lured it after him, away from his mate, and she can guide us safely."

They made much faster progress now, but they still hadn't gotten to wherever they were going when night fell. Dan threw his pack down hard, wondering if they would reach Maggie in time.

Over supper, Josh said, "Dan, don't be the gloom-meister you were back in high school. I want everyone to remember that *I'm* the one who first knew about the blue deer, even if I thought it was a horse, and now I say this white one is leading us right and we're almost there."

"I bet we get there tomorrow," said Alice. "This was task three, and the deers got us through, right?"

Everyone nodded. "Although that leads to the real task: Sister," said Graciela. "Any idea about her truename?"

"I'm working on it," said Dan. "And getting nowhere"— although he didn't say that part out loud. He explained how he thought the ring had flashed differently when he spoke Maggie's truename after Sister's, like maybe it was trying to tell him to use both names together. That would make sense, since they seemed to be merging so Sister could suck power from Maggie. But when he tried the two names again it hadn't acted differently after all. "Plan B," he said. "I get within bowshot of Sister, and I kill her."

"Could you really do that, Dan?" asked Alice.

He stared at her. "I'm a great shot," he said.

"I don't mean that. I mean, could you really kill her in cold blood?"

"Yes. I hate her." He didn't mention that he'd seen Mother Ferny use a shielding spell that blocked arrows, so maybe Sister could do that too. "I'll take first watch again."

THUNDER GRUMBLED ALL NIGHT, and when they awoke it was grumbling a little closer, but it still wasn't raining. The white doe stood watching. They stuffed their blankets in their packs, stuffed some dried fruit in their mouths, and followed.

Soon the ground began to slant down in front of them, gently at first, then more steeply. Birds began calling, and Dan realized he hadn't heard any since they crossed that creek. The white deer slowed, sniffed the air, and stopped. She stamped her foot, looked at them over her shoulder, looked forward and stamped her foot again, and then twirled and darted past them like a beam of moonlight. Before Dan could even say "Thanks," she was gone.

"Let's see where she was pointing," said Dan, "but move quietly."

The trees ended a few yards beyond where the white doe had stopped. Josh started to step into the open but Dan grabbed him and pulled him back. They gazed out between the trees.

They stood at the edge of an enormous bowl, covered only in grass except for an occasional massive Chattertree. Forest stretched all around the lip of the bowl that rose in the far distance to a height greater than theirs. At the very deepest spot, maybe a mile away, a stone tower rose from a smaller copse. Dan couldn't see anyone there, but they could easily be in the tower or obscured by the trees. He was sure that he had reached Maggie and Sister.

But someone was much closer. A short, stocky woman in a

long, black, hooded dress meandered up the hillside, sometimes higher, sometimes lower, but always drawing closer. She sniffed and muttered as she walked. Finally she called, "Come out, come out, wherever you are! I smell someone there. My Golden Lady has taught me a special name for a special boy, yes they have. Is that you, Dan, wandering in my pretty woods? Not going to let you ruin my comfy creepy rattles."

Dan would know that voice anywhere. Mrs. Westerley.

# RABBIT AND BONE

"*E*arplugs, Dan!" whispered Graciela. "Sister told her your Truename!"

But Dan backed up. "Jenny said they only work on Sister's voice."

"You get out of here, we'll capture her," said Josh.

Alice nodded. "She's too big for only one of us. So maybe this is why FCB sent us along."

Dan eased into the woods while his friends stomped through the bracken to divert Mrs. W. When he heard Graciela say, "Hello, Granny," and the reply, "Are you with Danny?" he began to run. Crashing and vague shouts broke out and then faded behind him. When he couldn't hear it anymore, Dan circled to the edge of the woods and peered into the bowl. Back where he had come from, he could barely make out figures that must be his friends and Mrs. Westerley, who almost seemed to be dancing together. Dan shrugged and looked in the other direction. A couple hundred yards ahead a tongue of woodland extended deeper into the bowl. Dan ran again, staying just

99

inside the trees until he reached the farthest extension of the tongue, and then peered out again.

There were no goblins or malkins or any other of Sister's creatures in sight. She must be relying on magic alone to protect herself if he got through the threefold task. Well, magic and the tower, which looked impenetrable, not a door or even a window on the sides he could see. It wasn't very tall, but who knew how deep underground its dungeons might go? And Mrs. Westerley had just made it definite that Sister had forced true-named Maggie to reveal Dan's truename, so she probably thought she had nothing to worry about.

There was a door on his side of the tower after all, because it suddenly opened. Dan backed into the trees as two figures stepped out. The one with long blond hair wore a black dress; the one with long dark hair seemed to be in some weird white outfit. Sister and Maggie? They were too far away to make out clearly, and black dress-white dress seemed corny, but Dan felt sure it was them. He scanned for any kind of shelter that would let him get closer unseen, but the Chattertrees were scattered too far apart to help.

Then the figures waved at him as though he stood in plain view. Either they'd seen him before he ducked back, or, yeah, probably magic.

And overconfidence, Dan realized. As he opened Jenny's box and fitted the plugs into his ears, he envisioned how this would go. He would march straight down the steep lawn. As soon as she thought he could hear her, Sister would smile and shout his truename, but he would only hear waves. Long ago he had pretended so well to be truenamed that he had fooled a witch, and he could do that again. He would slump and stumble closer, and then truename Sister. Then, finally, he would make her free Maggie. Then what? Kill Sister? Keep her a slave? Either one was better than she deserved. He'd decide that when the time came. The earplugs felt like water was stuck in his ears after a deep dive. Not a big deal.

Dan took a slow breath and stepped out of the trees. Just as he'd envisioned, he strode down the steep lawn. He could recognize Sister now in the black dress. In the white—Dan stumbled for real. Not a white dress, not clothing at all, but bones. Maggie as a skeleton, only her hair and eyes alive. But this shouldn't have surprised him; of course she would morph into skeleton form from all the pain Sister wielded. Dan grimaced and regained his stride. Sister smiled, just as he had envisioned. And just as he had envisioned, she called out his truename: "Círdan James Hillman, you are mine!"

Wait. Jenny had said he would only hear waves, but instead it was as though Sister had called to him beside the ocean; there were waves, yes, but the words were clear. For an instant Dan feared he had been truenamed, but that was stupid—if he were truenamed he would know it. The plugs worked! Dan slumped and staggered down the lawn, dropping to his knees, lurching up, and staggering on. Just as he had envisioned. And now he was close enough that he didn't have to shout, but shout he did, standing tall, arms upraised:

"Minik Mingarria!"

Sister just laughed her tinkly laugh.

After all that planning, all the struggle to learn her true-name, all that struggle to get here—she just laughed.

"Come now, Daniel. Did you truly think that after uniting my sister's power with mine I would not be able to block a truenaming?"

"She is not your sister," snarled Dan. Maggie should have said the same, but her skull merely lolled sideways, and her fingerbones twitched and clicked.

Sister laughed again but then frowned and said, "But why did my truenaming not work on you? Maggie could not have held any part of it back, and I have filled my valley with counterspells against anything that Quickfoot or Mother Ferny could conjure. No matter, I have many spells." She pointed at Dan and snapped, "Down!"

Dan's knees buckled, but he heard ocean waves roaring. The earplugs must be weakening this spell too, but he had to get away before it was too late. He looked sorrowfully at Maggie, who didn't even notice. Then he turned and crawled uphill. Sister called out angry words in a language he didn't know, and grasses began to wrap around his wrists and ankles, but he focused on the sound of the waves and tore free. A little farther and he was able to stand and run, run until he reached the trees, then run some more. He only stopped when he heard Josh shouting his name from back near the forest edge. In his terror and dismay he hadn't even noticed the pounding in his ears, but now it was like that time he had been boogie boarding and the waves had crashed his head into the sand, only ten times worse. He yanked the plugs from his ears and plodded toward Josh.

They were all there, even Mrs. Westerley with her hands tied behind her back and a gag in her mouth. Alice hugged Dan and said, "We saw it. We couldn't hear, but we know—"

Mrs. Westerley interrupted but whatever she said came out as grunts and moans. "Don't worry about her," said Josh. "Under that gag we stuck one of my socks in her mouth."

"At least it was a clean one," added Alice. "As soon as you truename Sister, force her to give you Mrs. Westerley's truename so you can make her forget yours and we can let her go."

Alice, being sympathetic. Dan vaguely remembered moments of sympathy for Mrs. Westerley, but he didn't feel any now.

"Can't truename her," he mumbled. "Her magic combined with Maggie is too strong."

"It's her necklace, Dan!" said Graciela. "Mrs. Westerley told us!"

Mrs. Westerly shrieked and lumbered away, but Josh easily caught her. "She's not too crafty when she gloats," he said.

Graciela continued, "Sister is wearing a necklace that blocks any truenaming. Take it off her and you're home free."

Dan brightened, but not for long. "She won't let me get next to her. She knows she can't truename me but she'll stop me with other spells. Jenny's earplugs weaken the effect but not enough."

"Josh and I will go," said Alice.

"That's crazy," replied Dan. "She'll hurt you. She can get your truenames from Maggie too."

"That's just it. Maggie doesn't know our middle names," said Alice. "Until recently we weren't that close. We saw you pretending to be truenamed; doesn't look that hard."

"She tried truenaming you first, right?" said Josh. "We think she'll do the same with us, but it won't work."

"It's still crazy. What if she just does one of her paralyzing pain spells?"

"She doesn't know we know about the necklace. We still might be able to get it off."

"No," said Dan.

"Anybody got a better idea?" asked Josh. "No? Let's go."

Dan tried to grab them but just then Mrs. Westerley made another break for it, and he had to help Graciela drag her back. Josh and Alice marched down toward where Sister and Maggie waited, seeming to welcome their approach. Dan paused to put in his earplugs, glad that the pain started out low again, and then he and Graciela followed with Mrs. Westerley. They stopped when Dan thought they were far enough that Sister's spells wouldn't work on them, but close enough to hear.

Sister turned and said something to Maggie, who lifted her skull and spoke back. Dan heard the faint clatter of her teeth. Sister smiled and shouted, "Joshua Gunther! Alice Mirlow!" She had fallen for it!

Josh and Alice fell to the ground, and Dan gritted his teeth. Overacting. But now they were up and staggering, and Sister didn't seem to realize that that it was fake. They were getting close. This might actually work! If Sister gives them a command, let it be that they stand nearby!

But when Josh and Alice were still a few yards from her, Sister pointed uphill and said, "Free my mother. Kill Dan and Graciela."

Josh and Alice halted and began turning toward him, and Dan had a flash of fear that they really were truenamed. But then his friends sprinted for Sister. Josh ran fast. Alice ran faster.

But Sister was fastest. She jerked her arms up and down and Josh and Alice seemed to bounce off a wall and fly ten feet backward. Sister pointed at them and they silently writhed on the ground. "Now bring me my mother!" she shouted uphill.

Graciela looked at Dan.

"Maggie," he said. "It has to be Maggie."

"What?"

"They're twinned now. Twin sisters. See how certain Sister is that she is invulnerable, just waiting for us and giving orders? I have to break Maggie free. She has to take off the necklace."

"But how?"

"I have one last idea. I'm sorry, but you need to take Mrs. W. You walk slow, and I'll try to be quick."

Dan began stringing his bow. Out of the corner of his eye he saw Graciela take Mrs. W by the arm and slowly walk her towards Sister. His hands trembled as he notched the taut string. Graciela called, "You plan to shoot her?" but Dan just waved her on. He selected his finest arrow and then reached in his pack for one more thing, the object that he had found under the floorboards in Maggie's room. He tied it around the shaft, and even though it didn't weigh much he knew he had to balance it perfectly so his arrow would fly true. He stood up and ran a little closer, then took his stance, left foot in front, brace on back foot, slowly drawing the string. Sister laughed and shouted, "Still a fool! Any arrow will bounce off my beauty, even if you can shoot that straight." The waves were pounding in Dan's head and he shook it as if to clear water from his ears. He aimed again. Graciela screamed, and he knew Sister had cursed her too. He had to recalibrate and aim again. And finally release.

Dan saw like everything was in slow motion. The arrow soared high, arced, and started its descent. Heading not toward Sister but toward Maggie! It clattered into her ribcage, and Sister shrieked with laughter. "No need even to deflect it! You would have killed your girlfriend if she weren't already dead! Círdan James Hillman, always a fool!"

"More fool you," thought Dan. The arrow had flown exactly where he aimed, lodging where Maggie's heart should have been. Her skull jerked down and her fingers jerked up, and she touched what he had sent her. Flesh grew around her eyes and she blinked. With her left hand she held it up: the rabbit's ear that she had saved after Mrs. Westerley cut up her stuffed animal, the magic toy that her brother the Prince of the Fairies had made for her to soothe the pain of Mrs. Westerley's tortures. Now she had a mouth, and it twisted in anger as she turned toward Sister and ripped the necklace from her throat.

Sister grabbed but its stones flew in all directions. Sister struck Maggie, and Dan heard bones cracking as she went down. Dan had been about to shout, but now instead in cold fury he spoke with a clear, flat voice:

"Minik Mingarria."

Sister froze. Graciela stopped screaming. Alice sat up, then Josh.

But something was wrong. Sister looked at her hands. She looked at Dan. She gestured behind her and Dan's friends fell and moaned. And just as Dan realized what had happened, Sister put words to it in a scream of joy:

"It has changed! My truename has changed! Twinning with my sister has made me anew!"

Then she looked at Dan with such hate that it knocked his breath away, and she screamed out, "Círdan James Hillman."

The waves protected him. But she walked toward him and shouted it again, and again and again, like a chant: "Círdan James Hillman. Círdan James Hillman. Círdan James Hillman..." And each time the waves quieted even as they hurt worse. All Dan's plans had failed, his friends were in agony, and he hurt so much that he couldn't focus his thoughts. He tried to look away from Sister and found he couldn't. Truenamed? He wrenched his gaze away and looked at Maggie crumpled on the ground, and she raised her head and gazed back at him. The flesh receded from her face, but just before her lips disappeared she smiled and pointed to Sister and herself.

And suddenly it was obvious. His twining ring had always turned green for both of them. In the woods it had flickered for both of their truenames. And now they were twinned. Sister was right in front of him, grinning as she prepared to say his name again, but Dan spoke first.

"Minik Maggie Magpie Mingarria."

Sister's face flashed with amazement, and then terror, and then went blank. She dropped to her knees before him.

"Now release Maggie."

Sister quavered, "I release you, Maggie Magpie."

"You will wait here," said Dan. "You will work no magic." He saw that his other friends were on their feet, and he ran to Maggie.

She sat slumped over, rubbing the rabbit's ear against her face. Flesh grew wherever it touched but melted away as soon as it moved on. Dan knelt and reached to hug her, but then twitched back, wondering if her skeleton was solid enough, and to his shame worrying what it would feel like. "You're free, Maggie," he whispered. "You can come back now. You're safe."

"Broken, too broken," Maggie muttered. Her teeth clacked.

Dan remembered the cracking sound when Sister had hit her and she fell. He could see a fracture line in her left femur. Maggie looked where he was looking. "Oh, not my bone," she said. "Bones heal. I mean me."

Dan heard his friends come up behind and had the sudden thought that even though Maggie was a skeleton, she deserved not to be nude. He pulled from his pack an oversized tee shirt and carefully slipped it over her head. Maggie didn't respond, so he gently lifted each bony arm and slipped them through the sleeves, then pulled the shirt over her pelvis. Maggie neither helped nor hindered. She sat with her skull tilted down and seemed not to notice when Dan put his arm around her shoulder. Dan's stomach turned over, or his heart was pounding, or something. None of those stupid cliches captured what he was feeling. His girlfriend whom he loved as a fountain of life and energy and beauty was a silent skeleton. Well, he loved her anyway, but he seethed.

Dan looked up to see Josh, Alice, and Graciela frowning. He

shrugged and rose to his feet, then bent and whispered to Maggie, "You're safe now. I'll be right back. Gotta deal with Sister."

He turned to his friends, feeling his rage rise like a pounding sea. He yanked out the earplugs, but his rage continued, and he said, "Yeah, gotta deal with Sister. I realized back at Gatemoodle that I could never, ever love her. That prophecy is cancelled. Look what she's done to Maggie; Maggie may never heal. I'm going to kill her."

"Dude—"

"Shut up, Josh."

Alice whimpered. "You too, Alice."

Dan stared at Graciela, who had hated Sister almost as long as he had. Her head twitched left and right. "No, Graciela? After all that she and her men did to you? Coward."

Dan strode to where Sister writhed on the ground. He knew what she was feeling: absolute, mindless, burning abjection. He could leave her suffering like that, that would be almost worse than death, but it was too dangerous; he would always worry that somehow the power she had channeled from First Changing Beast would enable her to break free. How should he do it? He ran one hand over his bow, and with his other hand gripped the hilt of his belted knife.

"Look up, Sister."

Of course she obeyed, but she kept her eyes downcast.

"Behold your judge and jury," said Dan. "You tried to control the Gates of Inland. For that, the sentence is death. You tried to rule Inland and make it racist and warmongering like Outland. For that, the sentence is death. Your men molested Graciela. The sentence is death. You tortured and imprisoned First Changing Beast. Death. You tried to kill me and my friends. Death. And most of all, you have tortured Maggie. For all these things, the sentence is death." He released his knife and nocked an arrow to the bowstring. "'Sister,' what a stupid name. You are not Maggie's sister. I don't care if you have both been tortured by your parents, she came through it Maggie, and you came through it a monster. You are no one's sister. You are no one's friend. You are all alone. You are no one." Dan swallowed. "Now look me in the eyes. I want you to see what's coming."

Sister stopped wriggling. She raised her eyes. The eyes that Dan had always seen sparking with malevolence and pride and piercing intelligence were now thick and clouded as though she were already the corpse he was about to make her. Dan drew the bowstring taut. Sister sat still, just looking into his eyes.

Dan fired, but in the millisecond before releasing the string he twitched so that the arrow merely brushed Sister's ear. Dirt clods exploded where the arrow pierced the ground. Dan swung his bow around his head and flung it as far as he could. He drew his knife and pitched it after the bow, shouting, "No matter how much she deserves death I can't do it!" He slumped to the ground and put his head in his hands, but he had only seconds to face his confusion.

"We forgot Mrs. Westerley!" shrieked Alice, pointing. Dan jumped up and saw Mrs. Westerley lumbering down the hill. She had broken free of bindings and gag, and she jumped as high as her squat body allowed and screamed, "You will release Sister, Círdan James Hillman!" She hopped from foot to foot like a deranged toad, croaking with laughter. "I win! We win! Sister will be free! Sister will rule!"

Way too late to stop her truenaming, Dan, Josh, and Graciela seized Mrs. Westerley. Dan saw Josh trying to put his hand over her mouth, as if that would do any good. He felt Alice hug him, saying, "Oh no, oh no, oh no."

"But I'm all right?" said Dan, so quietly that only he could hear. Then, louder, "It's all right, Alice. I'm all right. Guys, I'm all right!" Dan laughed quietly, then louder and louder yet, shoving his knuckles in his mouth when he saw Alice looking at him strangely. Vaguely he heard Mrs. Westerley shrieking, "Círdan James Hillman! Círdan James Hillman, you must fall down." He started to laugh again. Josh and Graciela finally subdued her, retied her hands, and shoved another gag in her mouth.

"Dude!" said Josh. "That Greenfang person has better magic than she knew. Those plugs must work against everyone."

"That's not it," said Dan. "I already took them out. Say my truename."

"No way!" said Josh. "Not enslaving my best friend."

"If it works, you can release me right away," said Dan.

Josh refused again, but Graciela nodded. "I get it," she said. "Dan's right. He'll be fine, watch: Círdan James Hillman."

Dan spread his arms wide and laughed. "Sister isn't the only one whose truename can change."

THE TOP FLOOR of the tower was a single round room, carpeted, with comfortable furniture. To the east was a short flight of stairs leading to a trapdoor in the roof. At the north was a fireplace, and Josh and Alice had located a woodbox outside, so the friends all sat around a crackling blaze. Graciela had located the well-stocked larder, and although no one dared to try cooking the mystery meats, she had pulled together a good spread of bread, cheese, and fruit. Dan sat next to Maggie and checked to see that the strip of fabric he had wrapped around her fractured femur was still tightly in place. He offered her a grape, but she just looked at the floor. He wasn't sure if fairies could eat when they were in skeleton form, anyway. He swallowed the sob that was working its way up from his gut and put his arm around Maggie's shoulder. After a moment she put her arm around his, and he smiled despite the hard bony fingers: it was the first time she had done anything on her own.

Sister and Mrs. Westerley huddled together on the other side of the room. A five-foot length of rope extended from the knot Dan had tied around Mrs. Westerley's ankle to Sister's hands. Dan had ordered Sister not to approach and not to let Mrs. Westerley approach, and to call out immediately if Mrs. Westerley attempted to untie the knot. Dan looked back from time to time and saw Mrs. Westerley glower at him, but he didn't think she would try anything.

"Dan, obviously don't tell us what it is, but do you know your new truename?" asked Alice.

"It's easy to guess," said Josh, rubbing his stomach. "I know it from when we were little: Doofus the Chump, you are mine! No? How about—" Alice elbowed him, and he sat back, chuckling.

"Not a clue," said Dan. "The Gatekeepers told us on our first trip here that a truename could change if someone lived strongly in some new way, kind of growing into the truename. I've done so many things since my old truename worked on me, you know, when Maggie and I truenamed each other..." He trailed off, thinking of fighting in the war, bringing Nellie Longarms back to life, traveling to prehistoric times with Maggie, freeing First Changing Beast, and now truenaming Sister and freeing Maggie. "I have no idea what made the difference, and even if I did I still wouldn't know what name that gave me. I guess it doesn't really matter, the important thing is for no one else to know my truename, and since I don't, I don't see how anyone else could."

"What are you going to do about—" Josh gestured toward Sister with his chin.

"I'm working on it," said Dan.

"Can't you just force her to stay in this tower forever?" asked Graciela.

"I could. But I'm not sure I can leave even her in truenaming pain." Dan felt Maggie hug him a little closer.

"Dude, you almost shot her to death with an arrow, and now you're Mr. Sympathy?"

"You haven't felt it. Being truenamed is maybe worse than dying."

"Why don't you order her not to feel the truenaming pain?" asked Alice.

"I don't think that's possible. It would make her head explode or something, you know, being given an order that made her feel what the order was forcing her not to feel. So—"

Suddenly, even through the thick walls, they heard a clash of metal and many voices chanting, "Ya Hoy! Ya Harrah Hoy!"

Dan ran up the stairs, flung open the trapdoor, and crawled onto the roof. Staying low, he crept to the western side where the noises were and peered through an opening. The sun was low, but there was still plenty of light to see the swarming shapes. He crawled back and almost flew down the ladder.

"Gragguts, goblins, kobolds, and trolls!" cried Dan." "Errr, like the college staff got new jobs as soldiers. Did you bolt the door?"

"Of course we did," said Josh. "What do you take us f—"

From downstairs they heard the heavy door crash open.

"Remember, Josh? Our arms were so full of wood..." moaned Alice.

Josh had retrieved Dan's weapons from where he flung them, and leaned them against the wall, and now Dan ran and seized his bow. But what good would that do against the crowd he heard stamping up the stairs? Now the noises and laughter had reached the landing below.

Dan whirled and cried out, "Sister! Make them lay down their weapons and do no harm!"

The door flew open. Gragguts leaped in, swinging a notched sword and grinning around a knife clenched in his teeth. A troll that Dan recognized as the STEM teacher, looking as angry as if he had just failed to get tenure, pushed in and slammed a club against the floor, cracking the wood. Cackling kobolds followed, knives out.

"Stop!" Sister's voice was quiet but firm. "You will hurt no one. You will lay down your weapons."

They stopped. They hurt no one. But they didn't lay down their weapons.

"What is wrong, Golden Lady?" asked Gragguts. "What have they done to you?"

"Do not answer," commanded Dan. "Order them to leave the tower and leave this land."

"Leave this tower and leave this land," said Sister.

Gragguts looked from Sister, to Dan, and back to Sister. "Nay, Lady," he said. "I see they have you in thrall of some sort. This one forces you to act against your will." He swung his sword tentatively. "I cannot hurt them, that much of your order I must obey." He shuffled backward. The kobolds had already left, and the troll was turning to go. "And we must leave the tower. But your words do not compel us to drop our weapons or leave this land." He spat at Dan's feet. "We will see how long a siege you can withstand."

Dan remembered the full larder with relief and then horror. "Sister! Command them to leave food and drink untouched!"

"You will leave food and drink untouched," said Sister.

Gragguts turned back from the top stair and looked at Dan. "That order too we must obey. Too bad for you that my hungry goblins have already taken or despoiled all." He laughed and left.

Dan strode toward Sister and shouted, "What is wrong with you, slave? You will force them to lay down their weapons and leave the land."

Sister whined and groveled. "I tried, Master, I tried. So much pain, fire in my brain, I am weakened."

Dan pointed at her. "Make. Them. Leave."

Sister screamed.

"Dan," came a quiet voice. Maggie, speaking at last. "Dan, she does not lie."

# NO WALLS

*J*osh's stomach growled.

"And that's after only one missed breakfast," said Alice. "But that siege won't really work against us, will it? Can't we just take Sister with us and you make her order Gragguts and all of them to let us through?"

They had been too spent the night before to consider their next move, but Dan had awakened early and was pretty sure he had figured things out. "That's too risky. We saw that Sister already couldn't make them put down their weapons yesterday, and as the truenaming continues any orders she gives may get even weaker."

Josh jumped up and started downstairs. "Which means I need to bolt the door for real, in case her order to stay away wears off."

Dan waited for Josh to return, and then continued, "But it's not that complicated. Remember, Maggie is Maggie Magpie." He turned to her. "If you summon your birds and send some to

Gatemoodle and some to the fairy capital, we should be rescued before long."

But Maggie shook her head. "Do you doubt that I already considered this? I cannot speak to birds while I dwell as a skeleton, and I am too broken to regain my body."

Everyone groaned except Graciela. "Dan, you are a slave-master, remember?" she said. "Sister has magpies too. Make her make them do something good for once."

"Sister!" commanded Dan. "Are you strong enough to summon magpies?"

"I think yes," she whispered.

"Then follow me to the roof. You too, Mrs. Westerley, she'll feel better if you hold her hand."

* * *

"How did you like Inland University?"

Dan almost jumped. Maggie was smiling faintly with the part of her face that wasn't bone. Maybe she was feeling better now that Sister's magpies were on the way.

"It sucked!" said Alice. "Worse than real college," said Josh. "I almost stayed anyway," said Graciela. They sounded nearly as pleased as Dan.

"I made it," said Maggie. "When she merged us to suck up my power, I was able to keep a small part of myself free. She was magically setting Gragguts and an army to wait wherever you appeared. I wriggled into her mind at a feeling we have in common. College envy."

"You and Sister envy college?!" blurted Josh.

"Just let her talk," said Dan. He felt excited and, weirdly, proud of Maggie for discovering the energy to engage.

"I was surprised too," said Maggie. She paused. "About

Sister, anyway. So I jiggled her spell to make the army into college people. I could tell she did not really know what college is, so I believed it would be silly more than deadly."

"It was still a little deadly, but the silly won out," said Graciela. "And strangely enough, the troll professors even taught us something. One helped us realize you and Sister were mixed-up together making the whole scene happen. And the other helped me remember something about Breaklock."

"That I have to return it to her father," said Dan. "After freeing FCB—done!—and saving you, and I mean really saving you, back to your flesh-and-blood self." He pretended the task didn't worry him. "And then we get married and I don't need Breaklock anymore."

"Thank you for college, Mags," said Josh and Alice together.

"Afterwards she choked away any initiative. I am sorry I could not help more." Maggie hung her head.

"You did great," said Dan.

* * *

FEELING COOPED UP, they all climbed to the roof the next morning after "a hearty not-breakfast," as Josh said. They were met immediately by hoots and yammering from the besieging goblins and kobolds. "Lucky you are that we follow the Golden Lady's orders, temporarily weakened though she may be," hailed Gragguts. "Else my archers would pick you off where you stand."

"This is worse than being inside," said Alice, stepping back onto the ladder. Maggie wrapped her bony fingers around Dan's hand, and as the others descended she sat with him where they were shielded by the low wall.

"Do you still love me, Danny?" she asked.

"What? Of course! Why—"

"Because I am a skeleton, without even the strength to speak with my magpies."

Dan tried humor. "If I'd ever made a Tinder account, speaking with magpies would have been way low on the requirements."

Maggie ignored him. "I know you loved me for my beauty. My beauty is gone."

"Of course I love your beauty, Maggie. Back in school before I knew you that's what I saw first and wanted. But now I love you as a person, or fairy, or skeleton—whatever! Anyway, the fairies and Mother Ferny will heal you." Dan knew his voice sounded weak, and his ending comment hadn't helped.

"You look straight at me without flinching as you say that, and I thank you for it. But I know you must steel yourself to do so. When first you rescued me from Sister, you drew back from me. And I do not know that I can be healed."

"It was just the shock of what Sister had done to you."

"I know you will marry me still, but instead of joyfully it will be dutifully, done to save Inland. And I will marry you out of duty, but also out of love, love mixed with grief that I am now... this." She tapped finger bone against boney face.

How could she be doing this? It had been a long time since they had this kind of argument, and it felt especially unfair after he had just rescued her. But then she voiced his own next thought:

"If only you had come sooner, perhaps I would be less broken."

Could he have come sooner? He had tried to hurry at every step. But could he somehow have dawdled a day less with Graciela by the love tent? Could he have pushed the others faster through the Chattertree Woods?

"And sex, Dan? All the beautiful love we have made in misty Inland woods and beside sunny Inland pools? Would you make love with a skeleton? Can a skeleton even make love?"

The image creeped Dan out. "They will heal you," he said. He reached for Maggie's hand but she pulled it back and scooted away.

* * *

As Dan and Maggie stood on the roof before dawn the next day, he felt the foot of space between them as though it were solid. By the sliver of moon on the eastern horizon he could tell that almost half of his second month was gone. But more immediate survival took precedence over that worry: they had been trapped with almost no food for two days now, and even being very careful with water their bottles were almost empty.

"What will you do with her, Dan? With Sister?" asked Maggie.

Dan pulled his eyes from the goblin and kobold campfire embers that encircled the tower. "I planned to kill her when I rescued you. That crap prophecy about loving her—forget it. She deserves to die, and I feel she's dangerous even under my truenaming. All that time she was channeling FCB's power may have given her some resistance. But when I had her at the mercy of my arrow…well, you saw I chickened out."

"Really? Were you being a chicken, or was it something else?"

"You hate her, don't you?"

Maggie shrugged. "Yes. But that does not stop us from being family. Sisters of bone and spirit she has called us, well aware that we have different parents. And it is true. I think the abuse we shared has made us more alike than most siblings who are

children of the same parents. Alike enough for her to merge us."
Maggie shivered. "You are no chicken, Dan. Think, feel; why
did you not slay her?"

"The easy part of the answer is that I felt sorry for her. No,
that's not right, I mean I did feel sorry for her, but more than
that I know what it's like to be truenamed."

"Yes. How many people have ever been truenamed? Many
have warned us of the danger of truenaming, and all who dwell
in Inland seem to know of it, but in all our time here we have
never heard of anyone else being truenamed. Only you, and me,
and now Sister. It must be vanishingly rare. And so it gives us
three a special bond. Usually that phrase means a nice connection, but 'bond' can also mean bondage. What is the hard part of
the answer?"

It took Dan a while to respond. "I just get a jumble. What
you said about her and you both envying college? When Josh
and Alice and Graci and I brought her to the regular world, you
were here in Inland so you didn't see, but part of the time she
just looked like a college girl. I could imagine being her. And
she and I are the only mortals who belong in Inland. My friends
come to support me, but they don't want to stay. But she wants
to ruin Inland and I want to save it, so I'm not making sense.
And you have magpies, and Sister has magpies too."

"Yes. Sisters." Maggie leaned her hard shoulder against him.
Dan put his arm around her and sighed with relief.

"I guess all this means I won't kill her. Doesn't mean I know
what I will do."

* * *

THAT NIGHT DAN couldn't fall asleep. Partly because of hunger;
he'd had hardly anything to eat since he felt guilty about

bringing Josh and Alice along and so had surreptitiously taken smaller portions as they divvied out the dwindling food supply. But mainly it was worrying about how to neutralize Sister without leaving her in the hell of truenaming. He crept quietly up to the roof, trying not to wake anyone; he thought he saw Graciela's eyes following him but she didn't say anything.

The air was still and prickly with humidity. Muted voices and occasional snorts of laughter came from the surrounding army. Dan stayed low and approached Sister. Mrs. Westerley was sprawled sleeping against the parapet. Sister was hunched over, face near the floor, swaying slightly side to side.

"What am I to do with you, Sister?"

She slowly raised her head and opened her eyes. "Whatever you wish, Master."

Here was this beautiful—well, beautiful when not true-named—woman calling him master and saying he could do anything he wanted with her. Dan was so creeped out that he slid back a couple feet as though he could slide away from the thought.

"I mean how can I keep you from hurting me and Maggie and Inland without leaving you truenamed?"

"I know not."

Dan had hoped she might have in her repertoire some spell that would do the trick, so he tried again. "Sister, believe me, I know from experience that it's direct orders that hurt the most, but I must be certain: I order you to tell me of any magic or any other way that would stop you from hurting us."

Sister flinched and coughed. "Yes. The oldest magic, the newest magic. Kill me."

"I'm not going to kill you!"

Sister met his gaze and one side of her mouth twitched. Light from the moon or a star glinted in her eye. Dan remembered all the times she had tried to destroy him or his friends. Even before he'd actually met her she sent a witch who true-named Maggie and tried to truename him. He had saved Maggie but watching her and talking about it afterward he thought he knew how bad it was. But he didn't, not until it happened to him. He really couldn't leave Sister like that. He again thought of her looking like a college girl when they brought her to New York—looking like someone he could easily have been friends with.

Then he remembered something new, accompanying her deep underground, through mud and water, into an ancient cavern, chanting with her words of rage and hate and hurt, sobbing until First Changing Beast slowly walked in, the giant Lion Man growling but unable to resist. He remembered weeping as he gripped the razor-sharp blade, begging the Beast to run, to make him stop, but the Beast just looking at him sadly as he made the incision and captured its blood in an earthen bowl. Did he nick his own finger and add drops of blood, one, two, three? The bowl swirled and the Beast swallowed. Did Dan bring the bowl to his own lips? He moaned and cried out.

"Dan!" Graciela was jostling his shoulder. "It's a dream, wake up."

Dan lurched up from the rough stone, feeling its imprint in his face. "Why did you do that to me?" he snarled at Sister.

She whimpered. "You did it, you! You caught my eye. There is no wall between my eye and the catcher. Give me a wall! Patch me, sew me together!" Her words degenerated into garble and trailed off, and she slouched face down on the floor like a reflection of how Dan had lain.

Dan shivered in the warm humidity. He looked at his finger, but that was stupid, he hadn't been with FCB in the cave, that was Sister, and that was past. He said, "Thanks, Graci—but I have to talk to Maggie." He hurried down the ladder, and nudged Maggie even though he knew she needed her sleep.

"What is it, Dan?"

"When Sister does what she does, how does she feel? Does she hate it?"

"Of course."

"Then why doesn't she stop?"

"She hates that more."

Dan gritted his teeth. He didn't know if he was angry, or sad, or full of hate himself. He said, "Maggie, I know you need your space, but I need you to hold me now." She took him against her shoulder, and even as he felt her hard bones he felt something softening inside him.

* * *

"Maybe the fairies think it's Sister's evil magpies about evil business. Maybe they shot them down and never heard our message," said Alice. The shouts and chanting from the besiegers were growing louder in the morning sun.

"And what's Inland's problem anyway?" asked Josh. "Goblins are supposed to hate the sunlight, and trolls turn to stone. I still hate this place."

Dan was so preoccupied with the problem of Sister that he had hardly considered this. "Uhh. The magpies'll get through." They'd better, since he didn't have any other plan.

But Maggie did. "I will go and speak to Gragguts."

"What?"

"He has seen me with Sister many times. When he sees I am still a skeleton it will be easy to make him think I am Sister's mouthpiece. I will tell him she orders him to withdraw with his army. Because...because otherwise you will slay her."

"Mags, that's crazy!" said Josh.

"Well, not completely," said Dan. "In fact, it's brilliant!—except for the Maggie-goes-and-talks-to-Gragguts part. I'll just shout it down to Gragguts."

"That will not work, Dan," said Maggie. "Gragguts is wily. He knows how to read faces and voices for motives—he outmaneuvered Crackerbones to become Goblin Leader, remember. He will know you are lying."

"Well, then, let Sister do it. I'll just order her to call down to Gragguts and say they have to leave on pain of her death."

"That will not work either. Sister already knows you will not kill her. You can order her to lie, but I do not think Gragguts will be fooled."

"Well, you know it would be a lie too, obviously. So why would he be fooled by you?"

"Are you so accustomed to my bone form that you no longer notice it?" Maggie chattered her teeth. "Look at my face and tell me what I am feeling."

Dan stared at Maggie. Between them, Alice and Graciela had come up with a summery dress and leggings for her. Maggie was taller than the other women so her wrists and shins protruded, but she didn't seem to mind; in fact, Dan wasn't sure if she wore the clothes for her own comfort or to spare everyone else the sight of her. But—her skull. Her face. "Uhh. Right," he said. "No expression without flesh and skin."

Alice spoke up. "So it's a plan, except I still don't see any reason for you to go down in person. Shout it down from here."

"I cannot shout," said Maggie. "My Outland self would be wondering how I can talk at all with no vocal cords. But I cannot shout in bone form."

"Then that would be a last, last resort," said Dan, smiling a little because Maggie seemed to be back in action, even if it was a crazy way. "We still have enough water for another day, so let's just wait for the fairies. If they don't come, I'd rather try to fight our way out than have you go down by yourself, Maggie. But before anything else, I have to figure out how to order Sister to do something that will make her permanently harmless so I can release her." He lost his smile.

* * *

THAT EVENING they sat around the fireplace, looking at the bluish mold on their last hunks of bread. "Maybe if we talk, you know, plan a little, it will give us some appetite," said Alice. "So Dan, can we help you figure out how to neutralize Sister so you can release her from her truename?"

"Any help is totally welcome."

"She still has some magical powers, right?" said Josh. "Because she used them to keep Gragguts and his band away? So why not have her cast a spell on herself that she can never use her powers for evil?"

"Yeah, I've thought of that," answered Dan. "But it sounds risky because of semantics. She probably thinks 'evil' means something very different than we think."

Graciela was nodding. "Like those stories where a genie gives someone a wish and then what they say gets interpreted completely differently. 'World peace' turns out to mean everyone's dead, or something like that. But then why not a spell where she makes it impossible for herself to do spells at all?"

"I don't know, it's tricky," said Dan. "It seems like that spell would have to be continuous over time to do any good. But maybe it would cancel itself, be one of the spells she couldn't do. What do you think, Maggie?"

Dan wasn't even sure Maggie was listening, but she raised

her head and said, "I am no expert in Inland sorcery, but that does feel right."

They fell silent. Josh said, "Let's toast this junk, maybe it'll burn off the mold." They stabbed the hunks of bread with their knives and held them over the fire. As they pulled the charred pieces back from the flames, Josh said, "OK, but we've still gotta come up with something to take our minds off this or I won't be able to put it in my mouth. I know! Let's try to guess Dan's truename."

Alice and Graciela groaned. Maggie just stared into space. "Come on!" said Josh, "I'll go first: Danny McDannyface!"

Dan moaned and collapsed writhing on the ground. Alice shrieked. Graciela shouted, "What have you done?" Josh stared with his mouth hanging open.

Then they heard a strange clacking sound. Maggie was laughing. "Rise, my love," she said, waving her arms like conducting a song, "for I hear no heroism, I hear no grace, in naming you Danny McDannyface."

"Really, guys," said Dan, sitting up and laughing. "I was just reacting to that terrible joke."

Without thinking they all chewed and swallowed the moldy toast. Josh looked at his empty hands. "Well, that worked at least."

"What about it, Dan?" asked Graciela. "Any idea what your truename is?"

"Not a clue," answered Dan. He got up and bowed to Maggie, thrilled that she was showing more life. "I thank thee, fair lady."

"Is it important?" asked Alice. "Maybe you're better off not knowing, that way no witch or any other weird thing can force you to tell it."

Dan shook his head as he sat back down. "No one can be

forced to reveal their own truename. It's a basic thing in Inland magic."

"How would you even go about finding out?" asked Graciela.

Dan stood back up and said, "You're all brilliant!"

"Umm, yeah? But what's got into you?" asked Josh.

"Even you, Josh, for starting this conversation. I think I know how to free Sister from the truenaming and still keep us safe. Now let me think it through."

"Well, me and Alice have been thinking, too," said Josh. "What's the big problem about releasing her? Once the fairy army gets here, which I'm assuming they will because otherwise we all die and I'll never get to make another bagel sandwich, once they get here, they can imprison Sister in some super-unbreakable magic cell. Then release her and voilà everything is fine!— What, Graciela? What, Maggie?"

Graciela was shaking her head. Maggie was shaking her skull.

"Yeah, I don't think I can do that," said Dan slowly, looking at Maggie. "Josh, Alice, we've met the King of the Fairies, remember what he's like? Letting the fairies imprison her would be giving her back to her abuser."

"Dan speaks truly," said Maggie. "The way my father treated Sister is at the heart of all that has gone wrong with Inland."

"Don't forget how Mrs. Westerley treated you," said Dan.

"That as well," said Maggie. "The abusers and their cruelties are entwined. But Mrs. Westerley no longer has any power to hurt me, I have no fear of her. I know not what my father the King might still do to Sister, however, and even if he did naught but put her in a cell, she would feel his power over her."

"And if she still suffered under him, Inland would still suffer?" asked Alice.

Maggie remained silent, so it was Dan that spoke up. "Probably," he said. "But I don't think that's even the issue. I can't free Sister from truenaming and then give her back to her abuser—it wouldn't be that big a difference."

"Dude, this is Sister we're talking about," muttered Josh.

Graciela put her arms around Josh and Alice. "Dan is right," she said.

\* \* \*

DAN AND MAGGIE climbed to the roof while it was still dark and leaned against the parapet on the opposite side from Sister and Mrs. Westerley. The stars faded and the dawn chorus of birdsong began. Dan remembered the old days, watching birds with his mother. He'd come a long way since then, hearing birdsong sweeter than any in Outland. Too bad his mother couldn't hear it.

"There," said Maggie, pointing a bony finger.

Even as a skeleton Maggie had eyes better than Dan's human ones, but after a few seconds he saw the dark shape flying toward them. Soon he could make it out as a magpie. It circled, croaked, and settled on Sister's shoulder. She didn't move until it nibbled her earlobe, and then she feebly swatted at it.

"Leave her alone, birdie," said Mrs. Westerley. She also swatted at it, and even though she had lost weight the last few days she was still strong. The magpie squawked and barely evaded her, then turned its bright eye at Dan and Maggie and walked to them. It croaked and chuckled and then flew off like a normal bird.

"My father's knights arrive at noon," translated Maggie.

"Then it's time for Step One," said Dan. "I can't stand torturing Sister any longer."

"Dan, beware Mrs. Westerley. I fear the two of them can still make some mischief between them."

Dan nodded, although he didn't really see what Mrs. Westerley could do. He crawled over to them and whispered, "Sister, look at me. Listen to me."

Sister's eyes were blank. Mrs. Westerley petted her daughter's hair and said, "Don't be mean, Dan."

"I won't," said Dan. "The opposite, in fact. I'm about to release her. But first: Sister, I order you to cast a spell on yourself binding your powers to my truename. You will be able to cast no more spells unless you know my truename!"

Sister had flinched into Mrs. Westerley's arms when given the order. Now she nodded and said, "It is done." She smiled at her mother, who flinched herself, looked puzzled, and then cackled.

Dan remembered Maggie's warning from a moment ago and started to ask what was going on, but then came a great shout from below.

Mrs. Westerley cackled again. "You stopped her power to hold off the goblins. They will come for you. Hey, you said you would release her!"

At least he hadn't done that yet. The problem wasn't Mrs. Westerley, it was his own soft heart, preparing to free Sister without thinking through the timing. Maggie had already started down the ladder, and Dan ran after her, shouting, "I'm an idiot! Everyone wake up! Weapons! They're attacking but we only have to hold them off until noon!"

Graciela was quick, dressed and with knife in hand while Josh was still putting a leg into his trousers. She pulled Dan aside and whispered, "We can't though, can we? Hold them off for hours?"

Something boomed against the door, and Dan remembered

how strong trolls are. "Probably not," he said. "But we'll try." He had his bow strung and nocked an arrow. "Everyone ready?"

"We will not fight," said Maggie suddenly. "I will go to them as I said before. I will tell them that you will slay Sister if they attack, and that you will swap her for me, hostage for hostage, and then release her truenaming. But they are liars who will break the truce as soon as Sister is free. You must figure out how to delay them until my father's warriors arrive."

"Maggie, wait!" shouted Dan as she skipped down the final rungs. "Tell them they must give free passage to Josh and Alice and Graciela!" She'd said he needed to figure it out, and he had the idea at once.

"What?" said Alice, and "We won't run," said Graciela, and "Dude!" said Josh.

The booming stopped, replaced by the creak of hinges.

Through the open doorway Dan saw Maggie walking away, a troll's huge hand at her back. It could crush her bones any time it wanted, but the touch looked almost gentle. Gragguts walked toward her, scratching his head. Dan ached to shoot him—he wouldn't miss at this distance—but he couldn't, this was a kind of parley, plus they'd be attacked and killed for sure if he did. He sensed his friends huddled behind him. Maggie and Gragguts were talking. Then Gragguts beckoned to a little kobold, said something to it, and pointed to Dan.

The kobold puffed up its chest and walked over. "Scrocklly thing," muttered Josh. It had a nose like a tapir that swayed as it talked. "Boss says listen. Says you can't hurt me. We know that bony thing is just a slavepiece of the Golden Lady. And it's just like a ugly bareskin like you to torture the Golden Lady so she can't talk for herself. So we'll do what she says and not attack. And we'll let your sissy coward friends run away. But just the same, maybe you're a stinking liar like most bareskins, so we'll hold on to the skeleton. Hey, can't hurt me, remember?" The kobold recoiled from Dan's rage-filled face and trotted back to Gragguts. The troll guided Maggie to a distant fire.

Josh pulled Dan back into the tower and said, "We are not running away. And what did you mean, we only have to last until noon?"

Dan explained about the fairy knights. "But I have to get the timing perfect. Once we make the swap I can shout to release Sister, but then they'll attack unless the fairies are here. But if I wait a minute too long the fairies will get here and they'll just run away with Maggie. So of course you're not running away, you're going to be my warning system. Alice stands an earshot away from me. Josh on down the road an earshot from her. And Graciela an earshot farther. Graci, as soon as you hear their hoofbeats, you shout and they pass the message on."

"Done!" said Graciela. Dan ran up to get Sister and Mrs. Westerley as the others took off down the road. Sister was so depleted that Mrs. Westerley had to half carry her, so by the time they got back to the door Dan could only see Alice, standing at her distant post. Dan beckoned to Gragguts, who sent the little kobold to negotiate. "We must make the exchange just before noon," finished Dan. "Bareskin law."

"Stupid bareskins. I will tell Gragguts."

And so they waited, Dan watching the sun. He'd gotten good at this during his Inland wanderings. When it was almost overhead he put his hand on Sister's shoulder and stepped forward. The troll guided Maggie forward. It looked like the same troll that had been the Humanities professor, but she no longer looked foolish; her face was savage and feral. They paused twenty paces apart.

"Ready," grunted the troll.

Dan looked up. The sun was directly overhead. Where were they? "Almost."

The troll shifted from side to side. "Is this trickery? We trade now or maybe I crush a few bones."

Alice was so far away that Dan began to worry she had shouted her warning and he hadn't heard. The troll was shaking its head and growling.

Then finally he heard Alice's faint voice: "Now!"

"Now," said Dan. He nodded to Mrs. Westerley who guided Sister forward. The troll released Maggie and she walked toward Dan. He saw Mrs. Westerley whisper to Maggie and snicker as they passed. Then Dan was hugging Maggie gently.

Sister had reached the troll. "You promised!" shrieked Mrs. Westerley.

"Minik Maggie Magpie Mingarria, I release you!"

Sister straightened, and her change was so complete that it was almost like black and white replaced by color. Hand in hand with Mrs. Westerley she strode toward Gragguts as he shouted, "Truce is over! Kill the fools!"

Goblins and kobolds clashed their weapons, but instantly Gragguts threw up his arms to silence them. Hoofbeats, hoofbeats on the road, very faint but growing louder.

"No time yet to kill the tricksters!" shouted Gragguts. "Flee by secret ways!"

The troll seized Sister in one hand and Mrs. Westerley in the other. Troll, Gragguts, and all bolted with amazing speed, and it seemed as though the distance to the Chattertree Woods shrank as they ran. By the time the fairy knights galloped into the clearing only the heels of the last goblin could be seen.

"What did Mrs. Westerley say?" asked Dan.

"She said to remember Sister's words: she has no walls."

# THE FAIRY CITY

*D*an rubbed his sore butt. Josh bent over, hands on knees, groaning. Alice stretched more demurely. Graciela seemed fine. Maggie was far ahead with faster riders.

Fairy knights had galloped after the disappearing goblins and kobolds, but some power in the woods had enabled them to escape as though they had never been there. The fairies had rapidly realized that Maggie needed some major healing—duh, it only took one look—and most of them had immediately turned back up the road after gently placing her in front of one of the riders. A half dozen or so—for some reason they were hard to count—had stayed behind with Dan and his friends. They had lunched on crusty white bread and slices of green melon that tasted sort of like cherries, only better. They were also given a cold drink that tasted so good Dan thought it was miruvor before realizing it was just the first fresh water in days. Then they had ridden until dusk. Dan knew it wasn't worth trying to figure out how the fairies had just enough extra horses for them.

The fairies gave them more bread and melon, as well as cheeses and ineffable sweets, then withdrew. Dan could hear them nearby, and occasionally see them; they seemed to form a circle around the friends, presumably for protection.

"How many more days of this riding do we have?" asked Josh.

Dan calculated to himself. "Let's see, after we sent the magpies it was, umm, on the fourth day that the fairies rescued us. But we don't know how long the birds took to fly there, or if the fairies had to deliberate, and I'm sure when they did decide to come for us they rode much faster than we are."

"Why don't we just ask?" said Graciela.

"They don't seem very approachable," answered Dan. "It's like they were with us but ignoring us at the same time. Anyway, I'll try tomorrow."

"Speaking of unapproachable, you've been kind of brooding all day, Dan," said Alice. "You never even told us how you made it safe to release Sister."

"Oh! Sorry. I made her put a spell on herself that she couldn't do any other spells unless she learned my truename. Which like we were talking about before seems like no one will be able to do. And it's obviously working because she wouldn't have let a troll lug her off if she could do something more magically glamorous. But still, there's, well, Mrs. W's reaction is what I'm 'brooding' about. She cackled when Sister cast the spell on herself. And then when they passed each other during the hostage exchange, Mrs. W was smug and whispered 'No walls.'"

"Mrs. W is just a crazy pig," said Josh.

"'No walls,'" said Graciela. "That's what Sister said when you got mad at her because of the awful dream you were having a couple nights ago. She said there were no walls between her and you because you caught her eye."

"Doesn't seem like there were walls between her and Maggie, either," said Alice. "You know, twins. And I'm not sure about her and Mrs. W for that matter. What would Dr. Green say?"

"Greenjack," said Josh.

"Whatever," said Dan. "He'd say that abused or suffering people sometimes can't tell their feelings apart from other people's feelings, or emotionally join with other people to try to feel stronger. But great, that's Outland psychology, I don't see how it helps us here."

"I bet she's trying to work some trick," said Graciela. "Maybe if anyone learns your truename she'll be able to sense it. So let's all not figure out your truename."

"I'm your man when it comes to not figuring things out," said Josh. "Except that it's time to sleep so we can ride another day."

\* \* \*

As THEY RODE off the next morning, Dan looked for a fairy he could ask about how long the journey would last. That was harder than it should have been, because although he could see them in front, in back, and on the sides, they were shimmery, and whenever he rode close to one it seemed like he or she wasn't there anymore. He tried spurring his horse ahead fast, thinking one of the fairies would approach to rein him in, but his horse seemed to be colluding with its masters, because after a quick trot that took Dan ahead of his friends it neighed, shook its head so hard it almost pulled the reins from Dan's hands, and glared at him.

After that Dan gave up—and suddenly one of the fairies was riding beside him. "Hello, Dan," he said.

Dan peered at the fairy. "Deneb?" Deneb and another fairy named Antares had once guided Dan and Maggie and their friends out of the Marrowland in search of First Changing Beast, and that included defending them from goblins and negotiating with a wild clan of dwarves.

"Ah, yes, my star name. You may still call me that."

"Deneb, it's good to see you. I—we—left last time without saying goodbye, after all the help you gave us. We really had no choice, but I apologize."

"It is nothing," said Deneb. "You were preoccupied." That was putting it mildly. Dan and Maggie had mutually truenamed each other so that Sister could not truename them, but it had turned out to be a cursed existence.

"Yeah," said Dan. "And I'm sorry about that, too. We were pathetic. Um, how's Antares?"

"She is fine. Healed from the goblin-gifted head wound, although they used some poison that left a scar. She rides ahead with Maggie."

"Well, thank you for talking to me. Can you tell me how long it will be before we reach the capital?"

"Maggie will be there today. At our pace we arrive tomorrow evening."

They were quiet for a moment, and Dan got the feeling that Deneb was waiting for him to say something else. He was grateful for someone familiar among the weird fairies, so he said, "It's nice that you and Antares came with the rescuers. How'd that come about?"

"We chose it so. To protect you."

"What is the danger, anyway? Gragguts and his gang are

gone, and I have incapacitated Sister—Sally Wandil. I would have thought the Marrowland roads would be pretty safe."

"Indeed they are. But has it occurred to you that a circle of riders may keep something in as well as keep something out?"

"What are you saying?" asked Dan.

"Do not ask me to be more precise," said Deneb. He whispered to his horse and almost instantly was lost among the shimmering riders.

"Did you find out how long it would be?" asked Alice, as she and the others rode up.

"We get there tomorrow night. But there's something else. That was Deneb--Josh and Alice, you know him from before. Antares is up ahead with Maggie, and Deneb says they chose to come to protect us. But it sounded like he didn't mean protect us from goblins or weird Inland monsters. I think he meant from the fairies. I think we're captives."

Whatever the truth of that, nothing worse happened on the journey than increasingly sore muscles. When they had once before been to the fairy capital, they had approached on paths that wound this way and that for no discernable reason, but maybe they were approaching from a different direction this time, because the road only curved or changed direction like it would have done in Outland, to avoid marshes or circle hills. On the evening of the third day, they entered a forest of sighing, resin-scented pine trees. The road straightened and was bordered by small boulders, most painted white but others shining with what looked like their own mineral nature. They heard singing and laughter from both sides, but only two fairies spoke to them. They were a teenage-looking couple who crossed the road and said, looking back at them over their shoulders, "Welcome to Springtime!"

"Weird," said Josh in a low voice. "They're walking on

branches and sitting on the road and saying it's Springtime when as far as I can tell it's the middle of summer."

"Springtime of their love, maybe?" said Alice.

"Maybe," said Dan. "But remember last time we were here they welcomed us to Autumn even though that looked like summer too, with flowers and everything? I think it's about the state of mind of the whole Marrowland. FCB was missing then, now I've freed them, so: Springtime! I hope. The only other thing we need is to find Maggie and Dr. Greenjack."

For the first time their escort grew solidly visible: three in front, four on each side, and Deneb bringing up the rear. Dan tried to catch Deneb's eye but only got a barely perceptible head shake in return.

Most of them had been here before and knew what to expect when they emerged from the trees, but still they gasped. They beheld a broad circular courtyard with white cobblestone paths wandering among lush, brilliant flowers, some familiar from Outland, others that they had never seen. The pine scent gave way to a spicey odor that should have been too pungent but wasn't. And in the center was the weird, beautiful palace. Its spires were too tall for its breadth, and slender spans of its glittery crystalline material looped up, down, and around seemingly at random. And as before, fairies walked along these spans without paying any attention to the fact that balancing on them should have been impossible.

Actually, Dan realized, one thing was different. Last time the palace had been green, but now it was blue with orange highlights that somehow blended harmoniously instead of looking garish.

It was all so breathtaking that they hardly noticed their horses being led away and two women converging on them from different palace spans. One of them had a much longer path to walk than the other, but even though they seemed to move at the same pace they arrived simultaneously. They also spoke simultaneously: "Follow us."

Their voices were almost hypnotically charming, but Dan hesitated. "Greetings, ladies," he said. "We wish to be reunited with Maggie Kingsdaughter. Do you take us to her?"

"Follow us."

Dan tried again. "We appreciate your hospitality. But we remember well from our previous visit that the doorways and locks of your palace are beyond the skills of mortals. The starry skies and scented breezes of the Marrowland delight us, and we will happily camp in whatever nook or grove you recommend."

"Follow us." This time their voices were accompanied by the thump of their "rescuers'" spears on the cobbles. They were escorted around the palace to the rear, where the women touched the blue wall. It glowed orange and a door opened where none had been visible. They followed curving passages until they were totally lost, and finally were guided to a chamber whose door as well was invisible until it glowed orange under fairy hands. Inside were three sumptuous beds, one more than king-size for Josh and Alice, two slightly smaller ones for Dan and Graciela. Down a short hallway was a bathing area and toilet. A large table in the middle of the room held many covered dishes that smelled delicious, and clear jugs filled with liquids of many colors. But the chamber was windowless, and when the door closed behind them not even its outline could be seen.

"Well," said Josh, "I'm usually the goofball who ignores what's important and says 'let's eat that great food,' and by the way I wish one of you would take that role and then we could eat that food instead of being serious, but since no one's stepping up: What do we do now?"

"We were so focused on freeing Maggie, and then on being rescued by the fairies, that we failed to consider the fairies arresting us," said Graciela. "I wasn't here with you before, but I met the King after the battle at Gatemoodle, and he didn't seem very trustworthy."

"We do know what needs to happen next," said Alice. "Dan and Maggie get married, with me and Graciela and Josh in the court. But where does that happen? Here? Gatemoodle?"

"And can't your therapist help us get out of here, Dan?" asked Josh.

"I don't know. Those fairies took him as a prisoner to the King, and they have a real bad history together. Maybe he's caught too. I need to talk to Maggie to figure all this out," said Dan. "But how do I get to her?"

"Wait, we don't really need his help, do we?" asked Alice. "You have that Breaklock wand that will open a gate back to our world or even somewhere else in this world!"

Josh brightened. "Don't do our world, much as I'd like to go back, because FCB didn't choose us to come back here for nothing. But sure, a gate to somewhere safe!"

Graciela frowned. "Except it didn't work when Dan tried it before you guys showed up in that clearing."

"And the fairies aren't dumb," added Dan. "They didn't confiscate Breaklock so they probably know it won't work. Let me try." He took Breaklock from his pack and concentrated as hard as he could, picturing the Goth Woods as well as Gate-moodle, but just like before the gate only flickered briefly, with nothing visible through either side.

Graciela sighed. "Well, back to Maggie. They must be healing her in whatever passes for a hospital or clinic, right?"

Dan shrugged, but before he could answer the door opened and a fairy walked in. He uncovered the dishes and they saw roasted fowl, poached fish, cheeses, berries, nuts, and dark bread and butter. Then he named the drinks. The pale red one and the orange one turned out to be ordinary strawberry and mango juices. Into an empty jug he poured two parts of the clear liquid and one part of the pale green. The mixture fizzed and turned silver. "For laughter," said the fairy. Finally he pointed to the bottle filled with pale gold liquid and said, "For calm and resilience." He bowed and left.

"Yikes, I remember the silver one," said Josh.

"Yeah, you got so drunk I had to carry you to bed," said Dan.

"I'll try a sip of calm and resilience instead," said Josh.

"Looks like miruvor."

"What?" asked Alice.

"That's Tolkien Dan again," said Josh. "Earning that name Círdan."

"It's an elf drink, and, well, if you drink it you feel calm and resilient," explained Dan.

Josh took a swallow of it, set down the glass, snapped erect like a buck private in the presence of a general, and said, "Two words: Whoa. Whoa-whoa-whoa-whoa-whoa-whoa-whoa." His eyes darted about.

Alice hurried over and hugged him. "You OK, Josh?"

"Probably. I can see the invisible door." He gently slid away from Alice, then walked over to what to Dan looked like blank wall and ran his fingers over it. "Not that it does us any good, I can't operate it." Josh began pacing back and forth.

"Josh, eat something," said Alice.

"Not hungry."

The others all exchanged glances. "We'll save you some, tell us when you're ready," said Dan. Keeping an eye on Josh, the others sat down and began to eat the typically sumptuous fairy food, drinking fruit juice and pushing the silver drink and the golden to the side.

After a few minutes Josh sat down, drumming his fingers and tapping his feet. "Not proud of it, but a few times I took Adderall to prep for exams. This stuff is hyper-Adderall. 'Calm and resilience' ha! Fairies are lying, trying to mess us up."

"I don't think so," said Dan. "That silver stuff is way stronger than Outland alcohol. I think their drinks affect us differently."

"Not meant for mortal physiology," said Graciela.

Josh took some deep, slow breaths, and began nibbling at the bread.

Although there were neither windows nor visible sources of illumination, the room gradually darkened. Dan got up and peered into corners.

"Dude, what are you doing?" asked Josh.

"Just checking. In the fairy tales, captives always get helped by like Rumpelstiltskin or a little animal."

Josh rolled his eyes. "I'm twitchy enough without you being a nut. This isn't a fairy tale. It's a fairy real."

They moved to their beds while stars appeared in the ceiling to give glimmering light. Dan heard the breathing of his friends shift as they went to sleep, but he was suddenly wide awake. So much had been going on since he defeated Sister that there had been no space to think about anything but what to do next. Now, on a soft bed after a good meal, it popped into his head: Did it matter that he didn't know his truename? Long ago when he first met the King of the fairies, the King had scornfully asked how mortals function without knowing their truenames —how did they know their purpose, how did they know where they fit? But that's the thing, in Outland it was irrelevant that their names were their truenames, or maybe their names only became truenames when they got to Inland. Which means he'd functioned without one for like seventeen years. "So it doesn't matter. Go to sleep," said Dan to himself. But the ceiling stars had circled halfway around the room before he finally drifted off.

* * *

DAN WOKE as the stars faded. He hoped the real stars outside were fading too, so that their imprisonment wouldn't mess up their biorhythms and sense of time. The others gradually arose and took turns in the bathroom. Josh seemed fine after last night's norivor, as he had named it. A fairy brought an amazing breakfast. Otherwise, nothing happened.

When the light seemed noon-bright, lunch was brought in. Good as it was none of them, not even Josh, ate very much. They just sat around quietly until Dan said, "I've been thinking. We really are going to need a helper like in the fairy tales."

"Oh, don't start again with fairy tales," said Josh.

"You know, Rumpelstiltskin, or maybe a mouse or a bird."

"No, no," said Josh.

Alice said, "Dan, you're being silly. In a lot of fairy tales the rescuer is True Love." She ignored Josh as he groaned and put his head in his hands. "You shouldn't be hoping for Rumpelstiltskin or mice. You should be hoping for Maggie."

Dan noticed that Josh and Alice totally did not play with the true love idea she'd just verbalized. That was too bad, because there was that prophecy that when he and Maggie—well, the mortal and the fairy—got married, it would be a double wedding, and despite their denials he thought Josh and Alice were the obvious candidates. But maybe Alice had a point. He'd actually been kind of trying not to think about Maggie, because thinking about her hurt. Partly because of her weird despairing statements about them at the tower. Mostly because he felt guilty about not rescuing her sooner, and sad about the pain she must be feeling that kept her stuck as a skeleton. Maybe they could get back to how it was before, when she was joyful and playful and sexy.

The door opened and they all jumped.

It wasn't Rumpelstiltskin or a little animal. It was a figure clothed in soft brown boots and gloves, silver leggings and blouse, and a green robe with a hood drooping over the face. "There you are," she said.

"Maggie!" they all chorused.

"Are you healed?" asked Dan.

In answer she briefly pulled back her hood to show her gleaming skull. "They have done no more than let me hide my ugliness. Malice is afoot. You know better than I that you are captive. They let me walk freely because they know I am too weak to go far. I demanded audience with my father to find what is going on, and he mocked me by saying he would see me only if I brought Dan, knowing that these halls are inscrutable to me. I wandered up and down and knew not where to open until I felt Dan thinking about true love."

Dan grinned at Alice and said "Inland!" and then gave Maggie a gentle hug. "Then let's go see the King," he said.

"Wait," said Graciela. "Can't we all get out now that you have opened the door."

"I beg you not to try," answered Maggie. "You would be swiftly recaptured and placed in a worse prison. At least now I know how to find you. We will return."

Maggie took Dan's hand and led him on a twisty journey, always turning into stairways or halls that trended upward. Eventually they came to the highest level of the palace. It was just as Dan remembered, with floating globes giving light, evergreen boughs on the walls, vessels filled with glorious flowers covering the floor, and soldiers with swords and spears appearing and disappearing among the plants. It was glorious, and Dan didn't care. He only had eyes for the figure seated in the rightward of two thrones, a tall skeleton clothed like Maggie but with hood thrown back.

"Well, well," said the King. "True love."

"Father," said Maggie, gesturing toward Dan. "I have earned your audience. Explain the rudeness of your palace. Why are Dan and his friends imprisoned?"

"Even before that, why have your healers done nothing for Maggie?" demanded Dan.

"The mortals are in no prison," answered the King, looking at Maggie and ignoring Dan. "I have heard of Outland prisons, and I do not think in my palace they dine on foul food or fear a blade in the back as they sleep. We are keeping the mortals safe. If you wish, I will open their door, and they may wander the Marrowland until they starve or encounter dangers they cannot manage. I doubt they could even survive a Wineland Boar, let alone a whelkin or grimlet."

"I repeat, why have you not healed Maggie?"

The King turned to Dan. "Yes, you repeat, like the tiresome mortal you are. Yet I see no reason not to tell you. A weary skeleton is hardly marriage material, now is it?"

"What are you talking about?" protested Dan, at the same time that Maggie said, "If I choose I can marry whether I wear flesh or bone. And I honor my betrothal to Dan."

"The two of you shall not wed," said the King.

"Is the King of the Fairies a liar?" asked Maggie.

"You set me the task of freeing First Changing Beast to win Maggie's hand," said Dan. "And I have freed them!"

"Truly?" asked the King. "Then where are they?"

"What season is it!" shouted Dan. "Last time we were here you were stuck in emotional Autumn, everyone said it, what season is it now?"

The King remained silent.

Dan darted around the room, trying to fix on one of the fairy guards, but they were never quite where he thought. Then, just as he gave up, one stabilized in front of him, and he demanded, "What season is it?"

"It is early in the Springtime." Dan was surprised to hear Antares's voice, but there was no time to greet her. He hurried back to the King.

Before he could speak, the King said, "Barely springtime. Better called Winterbreak. I must allow that you helped the Beast. But some part is still caught."

Dan froze, wondering what that could mean. Maggie said, "Father, it is time that I bring you news from Outland. This is crap. I wouldn't give a damn if Mrs. Westerley would let me get married. We've come a long way from this patriarchal pig business, and in that way Outland is the better place. I will marry Dan whether you will it or not."

Dan whispered, "Awesome, it's like being back in the Goth Woods with you," and Maggie made a sound that might have been a giggle.

But the King chuckled. "That is the royal spirit clothed in ugly Outland cant. But hill, nil, jack o'rill, things happen here the way they will. A princess cannot marry unless given away by one of royal blood. Your mother still broods at the Knoll of the Other and will not thwart me."

"Ha!" said Dan. "Speaking of Jack, and we wondered where he is anyway, but the Prince can give her away."

"Yes, Father, where is my brother?"

"Far away and not returning until far too late. I told him that

Sally—the one you call Sister—will have tormented you so deeply that you would lock in bone form. I told him that I could only heal you if he brought me the blossoms of Starmallow. And he believed! Starmallow is a toxin, it has no healing power, but it has the power to keep him questing far longer than the change of moon that will lock Dan into Outland, for it only grows for three days where a meteorite has fallen. The same soft heart that led him to try to break the Old Ways and interfere with the punishments your Mrs.—Waisterlee?—meted out. Such a fool. He fails now as your friend just as he failed then."

Maggie bowed her head. Dan was so angry that for a moment he couldn't think.

But then he laughed. "Wait a minute. You can't follow through with this, King. There has to be a marriage between a mortal and a fairy every ten thousand moons or whatever, that's one of your hill, nil, jack o'rill things, otherwise Marrowland and Inland, I don't know, they fall apart or something. If you stop us from marrying you cut your own throat!"

"Do you think Maggie is the only fairy? Why, you need look no farther than this room to see many potential brides and grooms. And as for mortals, why, you have brought a few with you, have you not?" The King laughed as he saw Dan blanch. "But nay, nay, I enjoy your fear, but the ones you brought, even the dark one who has some spark, are second rate. Perhaps I will keep them as spares. But the blood of the land is better strengthened by a mortal with strong blood. You would do, but I do not like you or your designs on my daughter. And I believe at the next Full Moon you will be banished forever. I see from your face that you know that well. No, you and your friends will not suffice. I think the mortal bride must be Sally Wandil."

"Are you crazy?" shouted Dan. "She's awful! I can't believe any fairy would consent to marry her, even if you order it!"

"Ah, you have failed to love her, I see, that is good." The King chuckled. "But you have done us a great favor by rendering her powerless. An unpleasant lass she is indeed, living with goblins and their filthy ilk. But we can catch her now, and even now my best scouts seek her. As for your fancy that no fairy will consent to wed her, you know not my power to command."

The King stood up. "Hold your tongue, for I know your next thought before you speak it. You think of Gatemoodle and that shifty Billy Portman, or whatever name he chooses now. And you may be right that a marriage could be contrived there against Marrowland customs." He turned to the guards. "What I said before about allowing the mortals their freedom is no longer true. And best to put my daughter with them. Feed them, give them all comforts, but do not let them roam. I have spoken." The King sat and threw his hood over his face.

There seemed to be a moment of jostling among the fairies as to who would escort Dan and Maggie back to the prison room, but two quickly materialized. It was Antares and a stranger. They went single file: fairy, Dan, Maggie, Antares. After they had wound down what seemed to Dan to be most of the distance, he heard Antares whisper something to Maggie. He looked back as Maggie fell to the floor. Antares seized his elbow and pulled him forward, saying to the other fairy, "The Princess has fallen. I have this one, please escort the Princess." The other fairy dropped back, and Antares whispered to Dan, "You must feel before midnight: what have mortals that fairies have not?"

"Huh?" whispered Dan.

"No time." Antares straightened and hurried Dan around another curve. Soon he and Maggie were back with their friends, magic door shut behind them.

# THE OPPOSITE OF TINKERBELL

"What does that even mean?" asked Alice. "'Feel: what have mortals that fairies have not?'" Dan and Maggie had explained that they were now truly imprisoned, but it looked like Antares and Deneb would help them if they could solve this riddle.

"And why would those two go against their King?" asked Graciela. "Can we trust them?"

Josh said, "I think so, yeah. We journeyed with them before; they were pretty cool. I bet they have more allegiance to Dan's quest and saving FCB than to the crazy Skeleton King."

"I think so too, and we don't really have any other option," said Dan. "But what did Antares mean? What do mortals have that fairies have not? I always thought it was the other way around: fairies have all these enchantments and wonderful stuff, beauty way beyond anything in Outland. Like Maggie." He winked at her. "I mean, that's why I want to be here."

"Isn't it obvious?" said Josh. "We have cars, watches, guns, all those mechanical things that don't exist here or break down if we bring them."

"But how does that help?" asked Alice. "Breaklock doesn't work so Dan can't go get any of those, and even if he could, like you said it'd just break down if he brought it here."

"And it's too obvious," said Dan. "Antares made it sound like we need to put thought into it. Plus it just feels too blunt for it to work in Inland."

They sat quietly fretting. Josh grumbled, "I'll tell you what mortals have that I'm grateful for. We have a lack of crazy creatures like Nellie Longarms and goblins and so on."

"But a lack is a way of saying things we don't have, it isn't a thing that we have," said Alice.

"Just a dumb comment," said Josh with a shrug.

"Hmmm, maybe not," mused Graciela. "There was something about lack being a thing in my philosophy class. But Maggie is our expert on being a mortal and a fairy both. Maggie, what say you?"

Maggie considered for a moment and then spoke. "I think that Josh and Graciela are on the right track. Before Dan brought me to Inland, before I learned that I am a fairy, I lived a bleak life." She nodded to them. "All of you who went to high school with me remember that I was barely hanging on to the edge, flunking class, taking drugs. At home, my—I almost said 'my mother'—Mrs. Westerley was usually drunk on gin, screaming at me, hitting me. I was so depressed. Because I did not know who I was. Because I did not have anything to believe in. But the depression felt not like a lack of good but like a thing, a blanket, a smothering fog."

"So what mortals have that fairies do not is depression?" Alice slid over and put her arm around Maggie. "I get it Maggie, how bad it was for you. But I'm, well, lucky, I'm a mortal but I was never depressed. At least not like that."

"Of course," said Maggie. "I meant only that a lack is a thing."

"But that's brilliant!" said Dan. "What we want is the opposite of Tinkerbell!"

"Dude," said Josh flatly.

"No, listen. It's what Maggie said about nothing to believe in. That's why I started seeing Dr. Green, I had what looked like such a good life ahead of me, but everything felt pointless. Why go to college and get a stupid job? Why believe in anything? Now everything is full of meaning, even being trapped here, we're in terrible danger but I feel so alive. When Tinkerbell was dying, she was brought back to life by people saying they believe in her. But people don't really. It's the opposite of Tinkerbell! What mortals have that fairies have not is we don't believe in fairies."

"That is right. Dan is right," said Maggie, nodding.

"Well, then great. But the assignment was to feel it," said Josh. "How do we feel that? Everyone think about Tinkerbell dying?"

"No, that will not work," said Maggie. "In high school, the only breaths of freedom for me came from the Green Goblin's drawings, or when he recited a poem. Art is imagination, and imagination can make mortals at least play at believing in fairies. Tinkerbell is art. Do not roll your eyes, Josh. Dan had fun thinking about Tinkerbell, you could hear it in his voice."

Graciela took over. "To feel what mortals have that fairies have not, we must each focus on what puts us in touch with the death of imagination. And suddenly the assignment is easy. For me, it is los conquistadores burning the Mayan codices, and modern turistas who wander through Palenque and see nothing. Or steal artifacts." She gave Dan a look that he was to think about for a long time.

"Is it cheating when it comes from someone else's life?" asked Alice. "Because I think mine is when I heard about your, I mean Mrs. Westerley abusing you, Maggie, and what Graciela went through with those Men from the Sea."

"Empathy is never cheating," said Maggie.

"And I think Maggie and I said our deadest moments a few minutes ago. It'll take a little work in the middle of fairyland, but we all know how to disbelieve in fairies," finished Dan.

"I don't," said Josh.

"Well, come on then, think!" said Graciela.

"Math class?" proposed Alice.

"Deadly," said Josh. "But no. 'Cause I always used it as a chance to imagine being anywhere but there."

"What time is it?" wondered Dan.

As though in response, the lighting dimmed.

"Night is coming," said Alice, "and time's running out. Josh, think! We won't leave you, but staying would be disaster. Dan, do something!"

Dan just glared at Josh.

Josh turned toward the wall and said, "I don't have enough hit points to survive that death stare, buddy."

"Footsteps approach," said Maggie.

Alice ran to Josh and took his hand. "C'mon, c'mon, Josh. How 'bout when we had that fight about your sweater, or when I yelled at you for forgetting my birthday?"

Josh shook his head. "I always imagined things would work out."

The door opened, and Antares and Deneb stepped in.

Antares spoke. "The guards will arrive at any moment. You must feel what mortals have that fairies do not, and you must feel it deeply."

"What will happen?" asked Dan.

"It will take you to…another place. Fairy but not fairy. From there you must make your way to Gatemoodle. It will be to your right." Antares pointed.

"Can't you guide us?"

"We cannot," replied Deneb, "since you go to a place that is not fairy. But harken to footsteps not two minutes away!"

"I'll try math class," muttered Josh.

Dan conjured memories he had easily avoided since first traveling to Inland: good at school, but bored and depressed. No Dr. Green yet. A crush on Maggie who was with the Green Goblin and had no interest in him. Basically he was an asshole and a loser.

He felt sick and weak. It was weird watching the others. It was as though a few sparks were blinking out around them, even though there hadn't been any sparks to begin with. Except nothing from Josh. And sparks or not, they were all still standing there.

"You must feel it deeply!" hissed Antares.

"Drink that stuff that made me crazy," said Josh. He strode to the table, took a swig from the gold bottle, and passed it around. Everyone took a drink, Dan last.

Electricity crackled up and down his spine. Sparks were flying and blinking out around all his friends—except Josh. Their feet seemed to be twisting and sinking into the floor. Dan looked down and his legs above his feet were out of sight. But Josh just stood there, eyes wide like a deer uselessly staring at the oncoming headlights.

"Josh, you complete idiot loser," snarled Dan. "You always fuck everything up, and I always have to drag you around and rescue you. I wish I never brought you to Inland!"

The last thing Dan heard as he dropped through the floor was Deneb shouting, "Guards! To me! The prisoners have vanished!"

The last thing he saw was a cascade of fire sparking from Josh and going dark, and Josh plummeting down past him.

\* \* \*

DAN WAS STILL on his feet, but the glassy smoothness of the castle floor had been replaced by knobbly roughness. At first it was pitch black, but either his eyes got used to it or a faint slime-green glow emanated from the walls. They stood in a dank passageway that stretched to his left and right. All his friends stood nearby.

Alice pushed him in the chest and whispered, "You apologize to him!"

Josh was staring at the floor but Dan was sure he could hear them. "No," he answered. "Let's move while we still have that drink in us that Josh gave the stupid name norivor."

"And now we have to follow the directions you stupidly accepted: 'to the right,'" said Josh. "Awesome, great, we were all spinning so which way was she pointing?"

Dan thought only a moment and then shrugged. "Inland. Antares said to the right, so it's to the right." He turned that way and took the lead.

The passage roof was high enough that Dan, the tallest, did not have to stoop, and wide enough that Maggie could walk beside him. After only a minute a passage branched off to the left. Maggie smiled and whispered, "Hey Dan, remember our adventure in the goblin caves, solving the dwarf shaman's riddle?"

Dan felt lighter, and he thought Maggie actually rose a fraction of an inch above the floor. He grasped her hand. "Don't cheer up yet, and don't get me imagining anything. Not as long as we're under the castle." He raised his voice. "Hey, everybody, these tunnels probably have goblins and worse things, so stay alert."

"Yeah, good job, jerkface," said Josh from the back. "You forgot your bow and arrows and like usual have led us to disaster. 'Let's go to fairyland and play in the slimy tunnels!' And how far is Gatemoodle, a thousand miles? If they even use miles in this stupid place. I wish you'd never brought me to Inland too."

Good, the faint lightness Dan had felt was gone. If there really were goblins it would be big trouble, but he didn't think Antares and Deneb would have sent them to a place like that. And the distance to Gatemoodle did worry him. But he was still full of energy from the norivor so he strode on, making sure Josh and Alice in the back didn't fall too far behind.

In the dark Dan found it impossible to guess the time, but after he felt like they had been walking for hours with no sounds except their footsteps and Josh cursing, he started crashing from the norivor. Since it had been the middle of the night when they sank beneath the palace, they had probably reached the next day with no sleep. He was just about to call a halt when the passage widened into a small room, and the greenish light shifted to a fungoid purplish color.

Dan said, "OK guys, I don't really think there's any goblins, because our friends wouldn't have sent us here if there were. But it was important to get a ways away from the palace before anyone cheered up. We sank because of dead thoughts, and

Maggie and I started to float when she got us thinking something good. I just said that about goblins to keep us miserable long enough."

"Like the tunnel isn't enough reason to be miserable?" moaned Alice. We don't have any food or water, and I don't know where Gatemoodle is but I'm sure it's far away."

"Right," said Dan. "I'm trusting Antares and Deneb. There is no way we could cover the distance to Gatemoodle on foot without supplies if we were aboveground. I don't know what they meant by this place being 'fairy but not fairy,' but it must operate under unreal time or distance. So let's just rest a little and—"

Graciela interrupted him with, "Is that a trapdoor?"

"Of course it is," said Josh. "A trapdoor to something awful. Giant spiders this time? Skeletal horrors?" He coughed and glanced at Maggie. "Sorry."

"Josh," said Dan. "About what I said—"

"Not now, Dan," interrupted Graciela. "We should get away from the trapdoor."

"Unless that's the way we need to go?" said Alice.

"It is not," said Maggie, with a shudder that rattled her bones. "It is not. Graciela is correct." She led off in the direction they had been going. Josh and Alice lagged behind, and Dan paused to join them.

"Josh, none of what I said was true!" he said.

Josh and Alice just glared at him.

"Oh, figure it out! You had to have something to make you feel dead! I insulted you to save your life and keep you with us."

"Doesn't mean you didn't mean it," said Josh.

"Of course I didn't mean it!"

"Doesn't mean it isn't true. What have I ever done here to help you?"

"Stop it! You're my best friend. The only true part of what I said is you are an idiot or you wouldn't have believed me in the first place." He tried smiling.

"You were very realistic, Dan," said Alice. "I think we all believed you."

Now Dan was getting mad. He stopped walking and said, "Would you rather Josh was stuck in fairy jail?"

"Now you're the idiot," said Josh. "Don't just stand there with trapdoor monsters lurking!" He smiled a little. "Do I always have to save you?" He looked back down the passage. "Run!"

"Ha ha, Josh," said Dan.

"Ha ha nothing! Run!" Josh grabbed Dan's shirt and Alice's hand and pulled them after the others. Dan looked over his shoulder. The fungoid illumination had faded as they passed, but he made out something moving jerkily in the shadows.

"At least it's slow," said Graciela when they had caught up. "Are we even sure that it isn't coming to help us?"

"It is not coming to help us," said Maggie. "I think it is . . ."

"Is what?" asked Dan.

"I am not certain. But I am certain that it is not a friend."

Alice hurried ahead, almost trotting.

"No, let's take it easy," Dan called. "As long as it doesn't start to catch up, let's just walk fast. Too easy to trip in the dark or miss something we need to see. Like loose stones we can throw." But the passages were barren, and Dan deeply regretted the loss of his bow and sword to the fairies.

"What about Breaklock, Dan? Will it work here?" asked Alice.

"I hadn't even thought of that, since we're still in the Marrowland—except down here maybe we aren't! So it's worth a try, but I have to stand still to do the spell, and then that thing will be on us. Let's see if we can get far enough ahead to pause."

But the thing matched their pace when they sped up. Once again they walked for what seemed like forever. Dan wasn't tired yet, but he was a lot fitter than the others so he knew they couldn't keep it up much longer, especially at this speed. He was just about to call a halt and suggest facing the thing, when Maggie said, "There are more than one."

Dan looked back but only saw the same jerky movement as before. "I think I only see one."

"They are coming. The horde."

With a sudden skittering sound the thing behind them came into view.

"It *is* a skeletal horror," whispered Josh.

Unlike Maggie, but like her father the king, this skeleton had remnants of flesh and tendons dangling from its bones. And unlike her father, this one had not hidden its rot underneath clothing. Alice screamed faintly. Dan stepped between his friends and the skeleton, although he had no idea what to do. He sensed Graciela beside him. The skeleton opened its mouth to speak, meat flaking off its cheeks from the movement. But the deep voice that rang out was Josh's, and the tune was Disney's Seven Dwarfs.

"Heigh Ho!

Heigh Ho!

Heigh Ho! Heigh Ho! It's off to school we go!

We learn some junk and then we flunk!

Heigh Ho! Heigh Ho! Heigh Ho!"

As Alice's soprano joined for another verse, the skeleton clacked its jaws together and shrank into the dark.

Dan burst into laughter, and finally choked out the words,

"Josh, my useless friend who never helps at all—right? Brilliant, brilliant, brilliant!"

Josh chortled. "I decided my superpower is being dumb, and the dumbest song I could think of might faze Inland. Ahem, I confounded its subtlety."

"Don't use vocab like that or you'll lose your superpower, buddy. Now let me try Breaklock."

Only Maggie showed no amusement. "Be quick, Danny. Josh and Alice have only delayed the horde, not defeated it. Still they approach."

Dan took out Breaklock and formed a clear image of friendly Gate Moot Hall, with Billy and Mother Ferny and even grumpy Crackerbones. The purple light around them changed to the earlier slime-green, with even flickers of leaf-green, but his gate sputtered, solidified only for seconds, and blanked out.

Dan was dismayed and hopeful both. Maybe it wouldn't work underground, or maybe they had to walk until they were no longer beneath the Marrowland, and that might take forever. But he knew better than to deflate the mood Josh's song had created, so he said, "That was strong enough to be encouraging. Let's get as far as we can before this horde is a thing, and I'll try again."

And for a while they were carried along by amusement. Josh suggested "100 Bottles of Beer on the Wall" next, and Alice said that would stop her progress at least as much as the skeleton's. Josh began the song anyway, but Graciela hissed, "Hush!"

"C'mon, Graci," said Josh.

"No, listen!"

Another side passage opened just ahead, and creaky voices were talking. A tall, thin woman and a tall, shriveled man stepped out. Their elegant clothes did not hide the fact that they looked about two hundred years old. Both looked straight at Dan as though his companions weren't even there.

"Friend! Fairy lover! The others have become dust and we are lonely. Join us."

"Uhh, no, not a friend, no," replied Dan. "Sorry. These are my friends. Guys, time to run again."

And they ran. Soon, though, hunger, thirst, and cramping calf muscles began taking their toll. Dan was sure they hadn't gotten far enough that Breaklock would work before they heard again the skittering of what they now knew was foot bones against the rock floor. And not long after that the noise grew to a clatter. Voices murmured, and Dan heard creaky laughter.

"Maggie," whispered Dan, "the dead are the fairies, right? So what are they doing in this place that Antares said was not fairy?"

"Not fairy but also fairy," answered Maggie. "I do not know. Something is wrong with them, but I know not what it is. Soon they will be many, and they will close the gap."

It was true, Dan could now see several skeletal horrors, and they were gradually closing in. He dropped behind his friends and said, "Guys, now is the time to run."

No one needed any encouragement after a glance behind. They were in a horror movie. Sore muscles were forgotten. Dan marveled at Maggie somehow running gracefully even though she was bones like their pursuers. The horde fell behind.

"A little farther, a little faster!" shouted Dan. "Then Break-lock again!"

Alice and Graciela sprinted ahead. Josh was only a little behind. Maggie stayed close to Dan, although he had a feeling she could skim past all of them if she wanted. Gradually the sounds behind them faded. Alice dropped to the ground and whimpered, "Sorry, Dan. Cramps!"

"It's all right, I think we're far enough." He pulled out Breaklock, and the lights around them shined with a pretty green even before he started the ritual. But he had no time. With a roar the horde of skeletons charged up behind them. He stuffed Breaklock back in his shirt and turned to face them. He could at least pull a few of them apart.

But Maggie stepped in front of him.

"Halt!" she cried. "I am your Princess, and I command you to halt!"

And they halted. The murmuring died away. But the faces of those with enough flesh were contorted, frowning. Bony feet stamped. One of the skeletons came forward, pushing others aside. It was shorter than most, but broader, with a square bulky skull.

"Princess!" he said. "Princess! Why do you come between us and our prey? You we do not want. Go in peace but leave the meat people."

"Who are you?" called Maggie.

"We are the fairies," called many voices. "We are the dead."

"As I am a fairy, and I am the dead. Yet we are not the same. What do you do here? And what do you want with my friends?"

It was the leader who spoke then. "We are the lost. You are unsure how to re-find your body." It tilted its head to the side, considering her. "You still hope, and as long as you do, you may find a way back to flesh. Or you may not, and then you will return to us for eternity, and you will understand. We are the stuck, the frozen. What do we want with your friends? Not to hurt them! We are lonely. We only want to keep them, to hear again what it is like to have flesh. There is no way out. Let us have them now! While they still have life and can speak to us of the touch of wind, the taste of food, the thrum of love. Alas! There is neither food nor water here, and when they are bones themselves they will be useless. So give us your friends quickly."

"You cannot have my friends. I am your Princess, and I command you to let us be!"

Others began clamoring. "But it has been long, long, long!"

"No meat people since the King married the Queen!"

"Only the old and dry!"

Finally the lead skeleton horror bowed its head. "You are our Princess, and we must obey you. But soon comes one whose command is mightier than yours. Flee while you can, if the sweet little one can even stand. You will not get far. We await the King."

Maggie took Dan's hand. Alice hopped to her feet, and they all strode forward as fast as they could manage.

"The King, Maggie?" asked Dan. "Your father will come down here?"

"I think not. Grandfather dwells here, maybe. Or Great-Grandfather, or an ancestor farther back. I know none of them. But I do not believe my father could have become such a creep without terrible parents himself. Will Breaklock work now?"

"Maybe. Let's get as far as we can. As soon as we hear a whisper of them back there with their King I'll do my best."

But Josh, Alice, and Graciela all shouted. The horde was somewhere behind them. But trouble was in front.

A tall skeleton with a silver circlet on his brow. It still had ropy biceps on one arm, rotting quadriceps and thick tendons on its limbs. Dan figured they could take him down and pull him apart—if it was just him. But a retinue of a half-dozen skeletons bearing swords strode up behind.

"I'll buy time," whispered Maggie. "Make a gate." She walked toward the King.

Dan pulled out Breaklock. The walls shone bright green, like a forest canopy on a sunny day. Dan composed his image of Gatemoodle and began the ritual.

Behind him he heard Maggie say, "Grandfather?"

"Welcome, Maggie Kingsdaughter," said a raspy voice. "No, I am a grander father than that." A creaky laugh. "You have come to join us sooner than we expected, though we have been aware of you since you locked into our form. You hope to rejoin the world and search for your flesh? I think you will fail, but I will not hinder you. Thank you for bringing the live ones to bring us joy before they flicker out. Especially him," and he nodded toward Dan.

Flicker out! The gate had looked firm but then it did just that. Was it because he didn't know his truename—no, that was stupid. Dan gritted his teeth. He had to stop worrying and concentrate. He heard Maggie say, "Before I leave, tell me of yourself. What fate led you to be King of the Lost? Who were the shriveled ones who singled Dan out? And what did the others mean about only old dry ones since the King wed the Queen?" The GrandKing spoke and Dan wanted to hear his answers but he shook his head. He had to concentrate! He pictured Gate Moot Hall, Billy, Mother Ferny, and Cracker-bones. The walls brightened. The gate formed! Formed, flick-ered, and faded.

But the walls were still green, and Dan called out, "Josh, Alice, Graciela! Touch the walls! Hold hands! Grab me!"

He had been standing in the middle and dimly he felt Josh grab him and yank him to one side where Josh could touch the wall while holding Dan's shoulder. Alice grabbed his other shoulder and linked hands with Graciela who touched the other wall. Green life, plant life, life from above coursed through them to Dan and Breaklock. He pictured the Hall, there! Billy, Mother Ferny, Crackerbones, there! A gate flashed and pulsed before him.

"Now!" shouted Dan. Josh, Alice, and Graciela jumped through. The gate began slowly to dim. "Maggie!" he shouted, but the GrandKing seized her hand. Without thinking Dan ran and made a sliding tackle. The GrandKing clattered to his knees and dropped Maggie's hand as swords flashed. Dan and Maggie ran for the gate, except one of his legs wasn't working right. Maggie dragged him the last step, and they were through just as the gate disappeared.

# WEDDING DAY

"**S**o what will you wear, Dan?" asked Alice.

"What?"

Josh and Alice and Graciela had been speculating about what Maggie's wedding dress would look like, but Dan wasn't paying attention. He knew it would be awesome because Mother Ferny had been weaving it for ages. But mostly he was enjoying just sitting with his friends on the sunny hill in front of Gatemoodle. He hadn't had much peace in Inland—it was all fighting goblins, fighting witches, staying out of the way of weird magic, and most of all fighting Sister. But now things had finally calmed down. His quests were done. He'd freed First Changing Beast. He'd defeated Sister. And soon he would wed Maggie. He lay back in the lush grass and took Maggie's hand. A real hand, flesh and blood! That was the best thing of all.

It was too hard to count the days since they had staggered through the gate into the friendly old Hall, but there had been many during which Mother Ferny made variations on all her best healing brews, and none of them had worked. Dan would have thought she was losing her touch except it only took her about two seconds to fix the gash in his leg from the lost skeleton fairy's sword. She kept muttering that she must be missing some ingredient but she didn't know what.

Then Greenjack had showed up waving a handful of flowers. Dan and Maggie had shouted at him to throw them away, Starmallow is toxic! But he had laughed and said he had only let the King think that was what he sought, he knew better than to trust the King, these were Moonmallow. He apologized for taking so long, but Moonmallow is even rarer than Starmallow, blooming only under moonlight when a Nightfinch sings, and Nightfinches only sing where Starmallow blooms. Or something like that, Dan had lost track. Anyway, it did the trick: Mother Ferny tossed it into one of her simmering pots and gave it to Maggie to drink. Maggie said it even tasted good, and then there she was in all her beauty. Only then had they hugged Greenjack and said how happy they were to see him, and told him about all that they had done since the Silver Guard escorted him away.

"I said, what are you going to wear?"

Dan sat up and said, "Uhhh."

Josh laughed. "Or me. Mother Ferny is making dresses for you Maids of Honor, right? Dan, whaddya think, Breaklock it to Inland and snag us a couple tuxes?"

"No," said Maggie. "Dan shall wear his questing clothes, raggedy as they are. I asked Billy to launder them, and that is all. They are the garments Dan wore to seek me and save me, and I honor them."

"And that means you're wearing your old junky clothes too, pal," said Dan. "Best Man can't outshine the Groom."

"More than fine with me," said Josh. "And you should carry

Breaklock because that thing has been crucial to seeking and saving."

"And soon I won't need it anymore." He winked at Graciela. "Don't worry, I remember the promise."

"About that promise," said Josh. I was there when Señor Guillermo gave you that amulet, remember. And yeah, he said Pacal would want his bracelet back. But Breaklock is pretty useful, and the old guy didn't seem super severe—"

"What is it, Mags?" asked Alice. Dan glanced over and saw tears in both Maggie's eyes. That had been happening lately, and it scared him.

"Pre-wedding jitters?" he asked.

She took a deep breath. "Oh, something the skeleton Grand-King said."

Dan felt a twinge of anxiety. In all the joy of being safe at Gate-moodle he had forgotten about the GrandKing and the peculiarities of the "fairy but not fairy" passage. He needed to hear more but Maggie shouted, "Fir Darrig!" She jumped up and pulled Dan with her. "Look, here comes Fir Darrig, and Turtle too!" She ran down to the road. Dan followed as fast as he could, but when he reached them Maggie already had her arms around the neck of the pony with the funny name, tears replaced with a wide smile.

"It's good to see you, Fir Darrig," said Dan.

"And you," answered the dwarf, bowing. Dan smiled; Fir (Mr. Darrig?) still had his necklace of smartphones that clinked together. "I and all of Inland honor you, for you have done much for all our land. When we met in the Inn upon your first arrival, I did not know what to think." He patted his pony. "Turtle was wiser than I and said you might be the one we needed, but even Turtle could not see clearly. I am glad it has proven true."

Dan thought this was the best part. Not the being-honored thing, that was kind of nice but mostly embarrassing. But seeing and greeting the wedding guests as they arrived. Crackerbones's wife Loosejaw had been the first, and like usual she greeted Dan with an affectionate pat on the back. His muscles were so hardened from all the travails of questing that he thought he would finally be able to withstand it, but no, she almost knocked him to the ground. Antares and Deneb had arrived yesterday accompanied by a dozen of the Silver Guard, all on magnificent blue and green horses trotting up the road rather than appearing through one of the mysterious fairy holes. Greenjack, of course. Dan wondered where Nellie Longarms was. He was a little worried she might not be coming, because Jenny Greenteeth and some of her weirder cousins were already down in the lake singing their shrill songs, but no sign of Nellie. But Billie said they still awaited some special guests, so maybe Nellie was one of them. Last of course would be First Changing Beast, and then would come the weddings.

Yeah, there was that. Plural. First Changing Beast had stated that this would be a double wedding, but neither Dan nor anybody else seemed to have any idea who the other couple would be. At first he thought Billy and Mother Ferny and Crackerbones knew and just weren't telling him for some sly reason, but after quizzing them he was pretty sure they really didn't know. Greenjack didn't, and he said he had checked with the Gatekeepers too and they just shrugged.

So Dan and his friends were making bets. Alice thought it would be Billy Portman and Mother Ferny. Dan couldn't see it, but maybe just because the thought freaked him out. Graciela was going with Antares and Deneb, and maybe they would make a good couple, but Dan and his friends had spent a fair amount of time traveling with them and they had never seemed lovey-dovey. Although come to think of it that was when Dan and Maggie had truenamed each other and were in awful abject dependence, blind to anything else. Josh guessed Nellie Longarms and Skriker the Doomcaller. That made Dan mad because Skriker was always moaning and that meant someone who heard him or someone they loved would die, and didn't Josh realize this was a mega-happy occasion coming up? And maybe a little bit of Dan's anger was because the thought of Nellie marrying someone made him jealous? But that was stupid...

Josh had answered, "Calm down, dude, just a joke. But all of you are leaving out the obvious." He paused, enjoying the moment as everyone stared at him. "Sister is the wild card. Sister and someone. Sister and Greenjack?"

"Dr. Green would *never* marry Sister!" Dan had said, reverting to the Outland name he had first known him by.

Maggie had added, "I do not think anyone would marry Sister."

"Still, remember what I always say. Two words: Inland. Sucks."

* * *

It was hard to keep track of time, but it was probably the next day, or maybe a day later. Dan had wandered down to the lake to look for Nellie, but still no one was there except her weird cousins singing their weird songs. Josh came up and clapped him on the shoulder and said, "Bro. You're looking all pensive like you're not sure about getting married. I can't exactly get a gang of guys together for a bachelor party, but I do have this." He pulled from his pocket a small vial of silvery liquid.

Dan smiled. "Is that what I think it is?"

Josh grinned. "Yup. I got Deneb to mix it up for me while we were trapped in the palace. But the first thing we've gotta do is get away from the lake and this dismal singing that would make anyone depressed." He led Dan down the road that Dan and Maggie had followed the first time they came to Gatemoodle. Out of sight of the Hall they sat on a bench in a sunny glade. Dan was certain the bench had never been there before, but whatever.

"I don't think we should drink that stuff, Josh."

"Just one sip each," replied his pal. "That's about all I have here anyway. Cheer you up a little and you can tell me what's bothering you. Alice and me saw you and Maggie huddled with Mother Ferny last night, and you've been gloomy ever since."

They drank. Josh immediately said, "Whoa!" and laughed. Dan didn't feel any more cheerful, but he did find it easier to talk.

"So it's something about 'fairy but not fairy.' Remember those two shriveled up people who singled me out when we were running from the skeletal horrors? And the horrors said something about 'only old dry ones since the King married the Queen?'"

"Nope. Don't remember. So you explain and then we'll finish the fairies' booze."

"The GrandKing explained it to Maggie, but I was making a gate and couldn't listen. Maggie finally told me and that's what we were talking to Mother Ferny about. The old shriveled ones were the King's concubines from before he got married. Mortals."

"So?"

"So in all our time together, Maggie and I never thought about how I will get old but she's probably immortal—you know, a fairy. We don't want to end up with me like them and her like, well, her."

"Oh. Ohhh. Dude." Josh put his arm around Dan's shoulder.

"But then Mother Ferny says it's OK. The mortal in the five-hundred-year marriage gets to age just like his partner."

Josh punched Dan in the arm. "So now you get to be immortal on top of everything else?! What's the big problem?"

"Well to begin with it means when I visit you and Alice in Outland I'll watch you age away from me, which will suck. Being immortal would be huge, I can't even comprehend it, how do I know I would like it? Maggie's always confused about how her Inland and Outland selves fit together, and now I am too. Fairy but not fairy, I don't know who I am any more. I wonder if not knowing my truename is actually a problem."

Josh sipped from the vial and passed it to Dan who swigged the rest. They sprawled back on the bench. After a while Josh said, "Remember when I used to believe in Sasquatches?"

Dan replied, "And then they turned out to be real!" They guffawed and spoke about old times until night found them.

* * *

THE NEXT MORNING Maggie smiled and said, "We go now to receive our rings." She took Dan's hand and led him to the causeway across the lake.

Dan felt a bit of a fool for not having thought this part through, and said, "I thought our twining rings—"

"Those are our engagement rings, given so long ago," interrupted Maggie. "Do not worry. I did not think we needed rings, but then my sisters called."

Dan flinched at the word "sister," but quickly realized she meant the Moss Maidens. And then he realized that the woodland on the other side of the causeway was greener, darker, deeper than it had been the day before. It used to be a trek to reach the Moss Maidens' grove, but now it looked like the grove had traveled to them. As they stepped under the boughs he heard song like the sighing of wind through pine branches turned into unknown words, like silvery beech bark made into music.

And he stopped still. The Moss Maidens had ensorcelled him with song long ago. But Maggie tugged at his hand and said "Come. My sisters accept you."

They wound their way around thick trunks of beech and maple and pine, and Dan did feel a little ensorcelled, but only in the way that he always felt good breathing in wild forest air—well, except multiplied by ten or twenty. Then they halted in a small grove. He heard the singing of many voices, but only one Moss Maiden materialized—had she come from behind that tree or out of the trunk itself? Iralia, the one Maggie had been closest with, had given up her physical existence in a Makeless Made to save the woodland from Sister long ago. Dan had never been able to tell the others apart, but Maggie bowed her head and said, "It is good to see you again."

The Moss Maiden reached into a pocket of her gown, kissed what she took out, kissed Maggie, and handed it to her. She then turned to Dan, reached into her pocket and kissed what she pulled out. Dan flinched back—it had been the Maidens' seductiveness that trapped him in the past—but she smiled and said, "You are safe, groom of our sister." She kissed him on the cheek and handed him a ring.

It was woven of silver filaments like twigs. As Dan gazed at it, it grew tiny leaves of emerald, and fruits of ruby. Slowly the gems dipped into the silver and were gone, slowly they grew again.

Dan looked up. The Moss Maiden had vanished. He slipped the ring into his pocket and took Maggie's hand. They walked back silently until they stepped out from under the trees. Then Dan said, "It's a little weird that we don't have any say in the guest list. Do you think your parents will come?"

Maggie shrugged. "I am not sure I want them to. My brother Greenjack is going to give me away, and that satisfies the fairy rule that it must be someone in the family. I do not need them. But it is not quite true that we have no say in the guest list."

"What do you mean?"

"You'll see."

* * *

AND THEN IT was the Day.

Dan wasn't aware of that when he woke up. He breakfasted early and went out to sit on a bench overlooking the road. He had a premonition that someone would be arriving that way, but the road was still empty when Josh wandered out a couple hours later. After praising Billy's cooking he sat silently beside Dan, also gazing at the road. Silent Josh was not a common version of his friend, so Dan figured he felt it too.

Then Mother Ferny stumped up and took Dan's hands. "Today is the day, boys!" she said with a smile. "The last guests have signaled they will be here any moment. Be at the arbor at noon in your wedding clothes. Now I must see to Maggie."

"Of course," said Dan as she walked away. "The full moon."

Josh gestured overhead and knocked knuckle against skull in the "crazy" signal. It was midmorning on a cloudless day.

"The moon's still up there," said Dan with a laugh. "I saw it last night just a sliver less than completion." He didn't mention that he had been down to the lake to see if Nellie Longarms had arrived. Only Jenny Greenteeth had surfaced to shake her head of algae locks. "Second full moon since I did Makeless Made to save Nellie. Still an entire moon cycle to go before I would have been banished!"

"And the wedding takes care of that," said Josh as they headed for the Hall. "Home free, dude!"

"And like you said, I won't need Breaklock anymore. But your idea that I should wear it during the ceremony—that would look stupid. I'll give it to Maggie; she'll keep it safe."

"Not sure why you still worry about it, but—hey! Who's that?" Josh gestured at the doorway, where a man stood dressed in an Outland tuxedo. "Is that—"

"The Green Goblin," said Dan. Then louder, "How'd you get here? And you said you'd never come to Inland; you were afraid you'd like it so much you'd never go back."

The Goblin shook Dan's hand, and with a smile and a "I'll even shake yours," he took Josh's hand. "I couldn't miss Maggie's wedding, even if you are the groom, Dan—kidding! And our old therapist came and got me, told me Mags wanted me here. Except I guess he isn't exactly a therapist, is he? Anyway, getting back? Well, Dave and I got married, and I know Dave's thinking of me, and I of him, and that will get me back."

"I'm glad to have you here," said Dan, and broke into a laugh. "I'm glad for everything today! I was looking for Maggie; have you seen her?"

"She's getting dressed, I suppose. Surely you know the groom can't see the bride on wedding day until the actual ceremony?"

"Who knows with Inland?" answered Dan. "But I guess. And we'd better get dressed too. I wanted to give her something to keep safe for me but Alice can get it to her—I assume seeing a Maid of Honor is allowed."

Dan shouted for Alice when they got inside and got her to take Breaklock even though she could hardly stop giggling about something going on with Maggie. Since getting dressed only meant putting on their worn questing garments, Dan and Josh were soon on their way to the Arbor. "You've got the ring, right?" asked Dan, looking over his shoulder at the road. Still empty.

Josh patted his pocket. "In the little case Mother F made."

Then they stopped. They would have gasped, but this was beyond gasping.

The Arbor was in the valley where the Battle of Gatemoodle had been fought, but any signs of the battle were long gone. Now golden grass grew there lushly. A broad alley lay between two tall hedges thick with branches and vines that twined around each other, seeming to grow and move although their size did not change. In the middle was an aisle covered with multicolored flowers. Benches of thick dark wood held dozens of celebrants—some old friends that Dan had already greeted, others unfamiliar weird-looking Inlanders in weird bright clothes. All of them were looking toward the end of the aisle where an outcropping of simple gray rock waited. Alice and Graciela already stood there, looking beautiful in matching blue and silver gowns, but Dan knew the celebrants weren't looking at them. He saw that beyond the rock the view somehow went into a great distance, much farther than an eye should be able to see. That's where everyone was looking. They were watching for First Changing Beast.

"OK, Dude, let's go," said Josh. As they walked down the aisle the blossoms bent away so none were crushed. Dan and his

Best Man smiled and nodded at Alice and Graciela and took up position at the other side of the rock slab.

Then the King and Queen of the Fairies appeared at the beginning of the aisle. So they had come! Dan figured they must have arrived through one of their magic holes in the ground, and they must be the mysterious last guests. Yuck, he almost wished they'd stayed away; Maggie's mother was a clean skeleton which was bad enough, and her father was bones and dead sinew and flesh which was even worse. At least they were mostly covered in regal robes. Billy Portman, Mother Ferny, and Crackerbones followed, and with her parents took the front row.

Billy winked at him.

But where was First Changing Beast?

Maybe it was waiting for the bride. But which bride? He still didn't know what the second marriage was supposed to be.

And then Maggie was there! At the beginning of the aisle and on the arm of—for Dan, the correct name was Dr. Green.

Maggie didn't need any special clothes to be gorgeous. But Mother Ferny had done herself proud. Maggie's forest green gown shimmered with crystal lines that morphed to sky blue and back again. Her velvet bodice was adorned with a golden sun in one moment, a silver moon in the next. Fireflies so bright that they were visible in the sunshine floated aloft from the flowing train. But to Dan, Maggie's smile and shining eyes as she gazed at him were the most magical of all.

But where was First Changing Beast?

Finally there came the sound of hoofbeats, and Dan relaxed.

Except they weren't coming from that mysterious distance behind the rock outcrop. They were coming from the road. Was that what he had all along sensed, that First Changing Beast would come by the road? Except why would it need a horse?

A flock of ravens red like fire burst between the hedges and twisted among the celebrants, knocking them from their seats.

Like smoke from that fire a white horse galloped down the aisle. Sister leapt off as the horse sprang over the rock outcrop and vanished, the view collapsing into normal distance. She had Dan's hair in her hand and a knife at his throat.

"I need no magic to train birds," she hissed. "I need no magic to ride a horse. And I need no magic to wield a knife. We have no walls between us, so look at me!"

Dan was strong enough to easily overpower her, but not when the blade she held was so close and sharp that it was already drawing blood. Sister held him between herself and all the magic wielders in the audience. Mother Ferny and Billy could probably zap her if they had a straight shot, but he didn't think they had any curving spells. He couldn't believe it! After everything he had done he was just going to be murdered? Everything was a waste? He thought he had wrapped up the situation with Sister by taking away her magic, and now she was just going to old-fashioned kill him? He had been so focused on Inland enchantments that now he was going to be a victim of mundane Outland violence. He should have killed her after all! And yet somehow he was still glad he hadn't.

He looked at Sister. He figured later that was what made the difference. And she had asked him to look, so maybe it was what she wanted whether she knew it or not. At first it felt like looking into the eyes of a cobra. A frightened cobra. A frightened woman. That college girl when she was in New York. The tortured child of a brutal father and negligent mother. It was probably only moments but it felt to Dan like they locked eyes for ages. And then Sister wept. "I cannot do it!" she cried. "After all, after so much, I cannot!" She dropped the knife, and then, bizarrely, hugged Dan. Feeling even more bizarre he returned the embrace, then took her by the shoulders and gently pushed her toward her skeleton parents. Except...

"Dude, look!" said Josh. He pointed to the front row. The King's disgusting rotten flesh and sinews dropped away, replaced by healthy skin. With a surprised face he pulled off his gloves and saw healthy hands. Flesh and skin grew upon the Queen, until she appeared as an older Maggie, with wisdom wrinkles but still beautiful. "At last," she sighed. "The curse is broken. Dan has loved both daughters!"

"What?!" said Dan. "I don't—"

Josh elbowed him and said, "Shut up! Don't mess with it, we'll figure it out later!"

Dan could hardly keep track of what was going on. The ravens croaked softly and landed in the hedges where they looked like overgrown roses. The King and Queen gathered Sister to themselves and sat her between them, on a seat that hadn't been there before. Crackerbones—Crackerbones who usually hated him!—asked Dan if he was all right. Well, Dan wasn't all right. Except maybe during his very first fight with a Noggle he didn't think he'd ever been so close to death. He was in shock from that, but even more he was in shock from Sister's mercy. Never, ever, would he have expected that. And the stupid idea that he loved her!

But Inland had bigger things in mind. Billy and Mother Ferny stood in front of the rock outcropping and began chanting. At first nothing happened, but then a great sigh went through the audience. Looking over the rock was like looking through a telescope that expanded to greater and greater lengths, until it again felt like looking into unimaginable distance.

Something—someone?—was out there, at first so distant that they looked like a dot, gradually growing larger, human-size, and larger again. Striding on hind legs, but the shape was wrong. It was the lion man, and now it towered above them on the rock outcrop. Dan had encountered it many times in Inland and the Shadowlands as he tried to complete the quest the Gatekeepers had given him so long ago: find First Changing Beast. Always in that form something had been wrong with the Beast; he had been melancholy, weakened, or trapped. Sometimes he had been she, a great black woman, and most recently he had been the woman and a huge lion at the same time, but then they had gone somewhere to finish healing. And it must have worked, because this avatar of First Changing Beast stood proudly and emanated power.

Dan hadn't known he was unsure, but a wave of warm relief washed over him. He really had completed his quest. He had found First Changing Beast, and First Changing Beast was strong. He tried to catch the Beast's eye and felt a pang of sadness when it paid him no attention.

Ah, but that was because it was here for the wedding, and Dan's bride was at the other end of the aisle. First Changing Beast raised its hands (paws?) and gestured to Maggie. And here she came down the aisle with a wide smile, and the flowers seemed to caress her ankles as she passed. The guests watched her raptly, and the only sound was a crack as Loosejaw whacked her mandible back in place. Dr. Green unhooked his elbow from Maggie, kissed her hand, bowed, and took a seat. Maggie stood beside her maids of honor, and she and Dan smiled at each other. His second quest, rescuing Maggie, was also complete. And now they would get married, and that would satisfy his Makeless Made curse and allow him to stay in Inland as much as he liked. And oh yeah, also satisfy Inland's need to have a fairy wed a mortal once every ten thousand or whatever moons or else there would be another disaster. Dan

179

loved helping Inland. But he loved Maggie, and being able to stay, even more.

First Changing Beast growled. Dan tore his eyes from Maggie to look. And First Changing Beast changed. In a way that should have been creepy but somehow was lovely, First Changing Beast stretched, and stretched, and split in two. One side was a giant woman of many colors. The other side was a giant man of many colors. And the woman was a lioness at the same time, and the man was a lion. Which was impossible of course, but no less true for that. Maybe it had something to do with the pulsations. Although there was no sound, and nothing moved, the Arbor pulsed as though with the earth's heartbeat.

Mother Ferny handed a ring to the woman lioness.

Billy Portman handed a ring to the man lion.

And the two Changing Beasts put rings on each other's fingers, and embraced, and kissed. And they did not break the embrace, but held tighter and tighter, and then they were one again. First Changing Beast stood there in Lion Man form and roared and shouted in a strange clanging language, and the wedding guests shouted in celebration.

OK! Dan and Josh looked at each other and smiled. So that was the other marriage! Josh drew his hand across his brow and whispered, "I told you, not me and Alice."

Dan and Maggie looked at each other and both mouthed, "Now our turn!" They couldn't stop smiling, and then they looked at First Changing Beast to learn how the wedding would proceed.

Dan hadn't seen it happen, but the Beast had changed again. Now on the rock platform stood the forms that he had rescued from prehistoric Africa: a huge lion and a great black woman. Back then the woman had mostly been laughing joyously, but she wasn't laughing now. She was looking straight at Dan, and so was the lion, and their expressions were warm and sad. And kind, which was hard to reconcile with what happened next.

The pulsations stopped and all was silence. The golden grass wrapped around Dan's ankles, and as he tried to yank free it rose to his knees and clamped him in place. The nearest hedge leaned toward him. Slowly, like a dream, vines grew out and twisted side to side as though they were searching. For him of course. Faster now they grew toward him.

From the corner of his eyes Dan saw other vines creeping toward someone in the crowd as he tried to deal with the ones coming for him. He swatted and twisted, but they easily dodged and wrapped around his body. The grasses released him. Maggie screamed. A man yelled—it was the Green Goblin. As Dan was borne away the last he saw was the Goblin being dropped into his place beside Maggie.

# REQUIEM

*D*an shivered. He found himself leaning against dank stone. Something nearby clanked and flapped slowly in the wind. Fog, he didn't know if it was in his eyes or actually around him, tattered and blew away. Gray clouds scudded overhead. He was in a courtyard with sad yellow grasses bending and whispering about the sun they missed. The stone was a crumbling wall, the clank was a bucket on a chain striking the top of its well. The flapping was a ripped pennant on a pole that leaned from a broken tower. Dan recognized that well and tower, and then the nearby structures: he was at the Castle of the Mad Prince.

Dan didn't feel princely, but he sure was mad. What in the world was going on? Why had he been magicked away from marrying Maggie? Had someone decided the Green Goblin was supposed to marry her instead? Who would be so stupid? The Goblin was happily married to a man. He and Maggie were good friends but neither would agree to become husband and wife. But maybe Inland was too ignorant or contemptuous of

Outland to understand that? And who was behind it all? First Changing Beast for some reason? Or maybe the King, he had never wanted Maggie and Dan to wed—but he had seemed happy about it now, even growing flesh together with the Queen. Because they thought he loved Sister as well as Maggie. How could this place he loved be so stupid?

The only way to answer these questions and straighten things out was to get back to Gatemoodle as fast as possible. But how? He'd given Breaklock to Maggie to store somewhere safe, so that was out. Well, then Kintravel. Dan wasn't very hopeful, though. The King had long ago forbidden kintravel in the Marrowland. Gatemoodle wasn't in the Marrowland, but whatever magic had spirited Dan away was probably smart enough to realize that it would be a waste of time if he could just kintravel back, so they'd have to get rid of kintravel too. But he'd try.

Dan closed his eyes and concentrated. It was easier than ever to conjure a true image of Maggie, beautiful in her witch-woven wedding dress with fireflies, smiling at him with joy. That smile, it didn't even really matter that Maggie had her incredible beauty, that smile from anyone was true love. He spoke the words.

And stood by himself in the hissing grass.

This had been a dangerous place before, and a weird one. He and Maggie had battled malkins here, and this was where a distorted version of the Green Goblin had beset them as a love-tormented prince, mad indeed. Now it felt empty, but Dan wasn't so sure he could trust that feeling. He hoped it was true, because he had been deposited here without his bow or any weapon at all. No pack, no food, and no warm clothing. Before anything else, he needed to get out of the wind. He didn't feel quite safe going into the castle, but at least he could circle to the lee side. Dan peered in all directions and hurried around the corner.

Nellie Longarms would be able to transport him to Gate-moodle via her magic underwater channels, but he couldn't really count on finding her, or on her either for that matter. He didn't know what was going on with her, or why she hadn't shown up at the wedding. He'd never understood how they became friends, and maybe they weren't friends anymore.

All right then, he'd do it the old-fashioned way. He had a month. He was pretty sure he was on a different continent than Gatemoodle, so he had to get to the coast and a boat crossing, and he'd check every body of water for Nellie on the way. At least he'd been here before so had some idea which way to go. The road from the castle quickly connected to a path they had followed. If he turned left, the path entered a great woodland and eventually reached a river where Nellie had dropped Maggie and him off. That was tempting; Nellie had been there once, so maybe she'd be there again. If he went that way, soon he would reach a side path that led to the Woods Witch's house. He'd skip that. There were other problems too, like the woods had wolves, plus trolls near the other end. But the main problem was that it would take many days to walk there, and he had no food. There were lots of streams so water was no prob-lem, but he needed to eat. Maggie had found delicious mush-rooms to sustain them, but he couldn't tell a good mushroom from one that would totally kill him. Not to mention that most of the shrooms they had eaten had probably only been good because Maggie magicked them.

He'd be better off turning right. That way climbed into foothills where they had encountered dwarf miners who had been friendly because they appreciated his quest to find FCB. His best hope of finding food was to get some from them.

Continuing on that path he would come to the pool with the three floating heads, weird women who had prophesied the future. Maybe they could tell him what to do. He and Maggie hadn't gotten much farther on the path because they'd had some stupid fight about something he couldn't even remember so she had run away and he had kintraveled out of there. But maybe the path would lead to shore and a ship. Or not. But he didn't know what else to do.

First he needed warmer clothing, and he remembered a lot of tapestries in the entrance hall. He edged past the broken door. The torches were burnt out and their sconces lay broken on the floor, but enough stones had fallen from the wall that he could see. Yuck, some stick skeletons lay there, maybe from the very malkins Dan and Maggie had killed. Dan relaxed a little; if anyone were here, they would have buried or at least removed the bones. And short swords lay beside the skeletons. Dan picked the one with the fewest notches and pulled its scabbard from the crumbling sticks. He didn't like the tapestries of the Mad Prince hunting, but found one showing a blue stag unmolested, cut it to size, and sliced the middle so he could fit his head through. An ungainly poncho was a lot better than nothing.

It had been noon at his aborted wedding. It had seemed to take no time to be transported here, so he should have a few hours before dark. Dan took a deep breath. Out the broken door, across the courtyard, under the portcullis, across the dried-up moat, down the entry road to the main path. Turn right and walk.

IT WAS STEEPER than Dan remembered. He was easily fit enough now to handle it physically, but it worried him a little. Inland was so weird that sometimes even its geography shifted; what if the cave wasn't there anymore? Plus he didn't have any rope to secure his makeshift poncho, so the wind that increased as he climbed higher flapped it around and chilled him. And it didn't have to be an Inland geography shift; a simple rock fall could've gotten rid of the cave just as well. All he could do was make his best guess, but as he clambered in that direction the ground became more broken, and in the last light he found himself at the edge of a ravine. That wasn't right. Dan swore and turned back, only to discover that he couldn't manage the jagged rocks now that the sun had truly set. He found a spot more-or-less sheltered from the wind and huddled his poncho around him.

The moon rose a little later. It was behind clouds so Dan couldn't see it, but he knew it was there from the way the sky changed from black to shiny steel. And the time of rising was right for one day past full, so at least Inland wasn't cheating him out of his last month, and soon there might be enough light for climbing.

Then he heard deep voices singing, above him and to the east, growing louder as they headed his way. He didn't know the language but it was the same that he had heard from the dwarf miners long ago.

"Hallo!" shouted Dan.

The singing stopped instantly. After a couple tense minutes he heard, "What be you a doin' down there?"

Dan saw a hooded face peering from above, and soon a length of rope dangled down to him. With that assistance it was easy to scramble up to the waiting dwarf. The dwarf looked at him expressionlessly and led him through the rocks to a trail that soon cut up to the cave. Torches flared as they entered.

"Wow!" said Dan. "You totally fixed this place up." On his other visit it had been barren except for a couple broken tools. Now it had wall hangings, carved wooden benches, shelves of blankets and fabrics, and barrels of provender.

"Times are better," said his guide. "First Changing Beast is back."

"And yer the one who found him," said another. "A great task, and now a complete task, so what is your purpose here?" There were six dwarfs in total, and soon there were six hands holding mugs of beer, but none was offered to Dan.

"Well, I have to get back to Gatemoodle. I'm supposed to get married there, only…" Dan trailed off. The twelve eyes looking over their mugs didn't seem to care.

"Your purpose is no longer our purpose," said the one who had found him. After a pause that was longer than needed to swig his beer, he added, "But we willna let ya starve."

The dwarves affirmed that the seacoast was to the east, the direction Dan planned to head, but none of them had actually been there—"It be a long, long journey." They gave him a rope to tie his poncho tight—"We have shirts and leggings too, but too short fer you kind"—and a bedroll—"That'll be too short fer ya too, but better 'n nothin'"—and a satchel stuffed with oat cakes and dried meat. Then they left for wherever they were going, and Dan fell asleep to fading song.

* * *

HE AWOKE AFTER A FITFUL NIGHT. The bedroll was as thin as it was short, and the cave floor was rough, but it wasn't really that. He'd come awake more than once feeling angry that the dwarves hadn't been friendlier even though they knew he was the one who found their First Changing Beast. Now his anger had cooled to a mixture of anxiety and sadness. If Inland didn't want him to marry Maggie and stay, did he really think he could get back to Gatemoodle and fix that?

At least he was warm and his stomach was full. When he stepped out of the cave, he saw the sun rising weakly through mountain fog. He started down the path but after a few steps turned back and searched though the dwarfs' shelves. They were rugged miners but their long hair and beards had looked pretty neat, so… Aha! He found a well-crafted wooden comb and placed it in his new satchel. Theft, he guessed, but too bad.

After a longer, steeper climb than he remembered, Dan reached the top of a ridge that extended northward. The high mountain that must be farther up there was hidden in fog. He and Maggie had taken the path up the ridge one time, and he was glad his goal now was in the other direction. Downward to the southeast lay the pool with the three floating heads. They had given Maggie and him useful, if cryptic, information long ago, and he hoped they could help again. Trying to reach the pool during daylight, Dan munched a late lunch as he walked, but the sun was already setting as he reached the edge of the trees. He had never been here at night and as far as he knew there could be wolves or worse things. He hurried on and then Yes! A faint glow ahead and to the right. He turned off the path into a glade with a phosphorescent pool in the center, and in the center of the pool bobbed three round shapes. Dan crept to shore and watched and waited. The shapes did not speak; were they sleeping? Were they even the same women's heads? Dan had to assume so and he didn't want to make them mad if they didn't want to be disturbed. Even if the woods was creepy, this glowing glade seemed safe. He spread his bedroll in a dry spot and went to sleep.

Dan was awakened by something soft and warm nuzzling

his ear. In all the books and movies the nuzzled person would think it was his lover, and sometimes it was and sometimes it wasn't. Dan had no illusions that this was Maggie, but it didn't vibe dangerous either. He opened his eyes slowly.

It was the white doe. *A* white doe anyway, but Dan was somehow certain it was the same one that had helped them through the Chattertree Woods, the one that was mated with the great blue stag that had secured victory at the Battle of Gatemoodle. He wanted to ask her why she was there, but when she saw him looking the doe pronked backwards and melted into the woods.

The three globes still floated in the pool, and yes, it was the same three women's heads. A blonde, a brunette, and a redhead. Dan didn't usually super pay attention to women's hair color, but it seemed to mean a lot to these ladies. Last time he and Maggie were here they had called out, "Hold me! Pet me! Comb my flaxen/raven/chestnut tresses!" He had recoiled when he waded out to them and discovered they really had no bodies hidden under the surface, but they had been happy to be picked up and carried like beach balls. He'd had Maggie's comb then, and when the tangles were too bad for a comb Maggie had taught him how to loosen them with his fingers. If he hadn't learned anything else in Inland, he had learned that; Dan snorted at the thought. But this time should go better. He took the dwarfs' comb from his pack and walked to water's edge.

Silence. As before, the heads seemed to float aimlessly, rolling in the water so that occasionally their faces submerged for a long time before rolling back into the air. Dan wondered if they even needed to breathe. They stared in all directions with their big googly eyes, seeming equally interested—or disinterested—in all directions, including straight in the air.

From time to time their gazes met Dan's eyes, but they paid no more attention to him than to trees and rocks.

"Hey, ladies, look what I have," called Dan, holding up the comb. "Is your hair tangled? This will fix it easy!"

Silence.

Eventually, hunger led Dan back to his satchel and oat cakes. He had an idea, swallowed a last bite, and returned to the pool.

"Hey look! I left the comb behind. Maybe you don't like it because I took it without permission, or maybe you just like finger-combing, but please talk to me! I need your wisdom."

Silence.

Dan got madder and more anxious as the day passed. By late morning the sun was high enough to reach above the fogbank that circled the pool but left the sky above clear and blue. By midafternoon it was sinking into the fog on the western side.

Dan grabbed the comb and stomped into the pool, creating waves that caused the heads to spin and dip, but their goofy smiles and googly eyes did not change. "I need to know what's going on with Maggie! I need to know what I can do to fix things! I'm going to comb your hair and you can talk to me!" he shouted. The redhead was nearest and Dan reached out to grab her.

And stopped. Nonconsensual hair combing, yuck. Not that she seemed to care; she looked right through him and floated away.

Dan groaned and gently set the comb on the surface of the water. "I know you guys don't have hands, but maybe you can use this in some weird magical way. Anyhow, I don't need it. Oh, and actually your hair is beautiful just like it is."

\* \* \*

THE NEXT MORNING, as Dan was about to step out of the warm comfort of the phosphorescent glade into the sodden woods, he looked back and called, "I'm about to leave," and paused for an answer. They floated on, always indifferent. Dan shook his head and called, "Goodbye, ladies."

Was it eternally wet here? Last time it had been pouring rain and the path was mud. It wasn't that bad now, but the trees were so soaked by fog that they dripped dismally, including on Dan's hatless head. At least this part was downhill. He soon reached the spot where he and Maggie had their big stupid fight and she ran off and he kintraveled to Josh. New territory ahead.

Not that it changed much, other than the fog thinning to a mist, and the gradient slowly leveling out. Big dark trees all around. Big mushrooms, some bright red, some white as bone, and some gray mushy ones that made Dan think of decaying flesh. He listened for howls and watched for movement, but not even a squirrel or a bird showed itself. Dan intended to head basically east, the direction the path had started, but he had no way to determine direction now. The sun was hidden, and moss grew on all sides of the trees. Dan wondered who had made this path, and hoped he wouldn't meet them.

Suddenly, right in front of him, noise: clinking and clacking. Dan froze and tried to spot whatever it was, but the path took a turn just ahead, and the noise came from just past the bend. Dan thought about circling around and rejoining the path farther ahead, but he had learned from Mirkwood as a young child that leaving the path made big trouble, and as a teenager World of Warcraft had only reinforced that awareness. Plus he had an idea who this might be. He walked forward quietly and peered around the curve.

Seated on a low branch over the trail was a little man. The

jingling and clattering came from bells and bones tied into his long, ragged hair and beard. Yup, it was Question Gnome. Dan hated this guy, because he only responded to questions, and only answered them with obscure questions of his own. But hey, any response would be better than he got from the floating heads.

"Will this trail take me to the coast?" he asked.

The gnome nodded and shook his head, which was useless except to his noisemakers, and responded, "Why do you ask questions that have no import for Inland?"

Wet, tired, and discouraged, this pissed Dan off. "I found First Changing Beast! I am going to marry the fairy princess! What do you mean, 'no import for Inland'?"

"Will you also waste your third and final question?"

For a moment Dan wished he had a rock to bean the little guy. But in addition to this being totally childish, it might provoke the gnome into zapping him with some special gnome curse. OK, OK, what was a question that would help him and for sure had import for Inland?

"What's going on at Gatemoodle?"

"Is what the goblin says true?"

"What goblin? Crackerbones? What did he say? Or Loose-jaw? Wait!"

But Question Gnome was gone.

Dan stomped on down the trail. That answer had been worse than nothing, tantalizing him without making anything clear, not even whether whatever goblin had said something good or terrible, so he couldn't even care if it were true... Josh always said that Inland sucked, and Dan was starting to really think he was right. He needed some sign of hope.

Then the trail petered out.

It was getting dark, he was wet, everything was wet, and

now wind began blowing down from the mountain to make him even colder. Staying in sight of the trail, Dan found an especially massive tree and leaned against the lee side. Then he stood back up, searched around until he found a thick stick a couple feet long and took that back to his windbreak tree. A cudgel, just in case. He gnawed on dried meat and noticed that at least the wind was blowing away the last of the mist. And then one of those things happened that made his heart beat for Inland; he realized that he could see the starry heaven even though he still saw the intervening canopy. Impossible, but who cares! And as the stars brightened the leaves soaked in their light and all the edges and veins ran silver. Dan shivered. Inland didn't suck. But his time was running out.

Dan didn't remember falling asleep, but he jolted awake. Something snorted. He grasped his cudgel and slid upright, his back against the tree.

The snort came again, closer now, and Dan raised his stick.

Then the blue stag stepped into view. Starlight sizzled up and down his antlers, and his eyes flashed silver. He stamped once, turned, and looked back over his shoulder before pacing away. Dan followed.

So long ago when he traveled these woods with Maggie, the stag had silently led them to an idyllic glade. Dan had a spurt of hope that the stag would lead him to Maggie now. How he longed to be with her! He didn't really care about getting married, they were only doing that because Inland's weird curses made it necessary. All he wanted was to be with his magical girlfriend in the magical world.

Dan no longer had any idea of direction, but he trusted the blue deer. Even though they walked in pathless forest the footing was easy, no sticks or rocks or underbrush tripping him. Maybe the deer had the same power to temporarily displace obstacles as the wodewose—Josh's sasquatch—that had led him and Josh and Alice through a woodland long ago.

Dan heard splashing water, and the deer led him across and then alongside a cheerful stream. The path steepened, and the stream gurgled and chuckled down small waterfalls. The deer stamped hard three times and sprang away. Dawn was brightening, and Dan saw that he stood before a great lawn at the end of the forest. In the center of the lawn glistened a lake, and just where the stream spread into it stood a woman. Dan was about to call out "Maggie!" when he realized she was too tall. And her hair was blond. And her arms were way, way too long.

She held those arms out to him and spoke.

"Dan has wandered far astray, Gatemoodle sent him away. Much better here, much better this. Dan has come for Nellie's kiss."

Dan strode forward, and they kissed, and Nellie pulled him under.

SKY BLUE, sapphire blue, midnight blue. Water breath cool and fresh in his lungs. Fronds and flashing salmon. Water nuzzling, scolding, caressing, entangling, releasing. Dan knew without being reminded to hold tight to Nellie's hand as she guided them through her impossible waterways. Now and then they swam dark grottoes and deep, sullen trenches. Then and now they swam swift rivers and wide lakes with forested shores. Nellie undulated around waterspouts and whirlpools, through rapids, and beside singing whales. On and on. Dan slept, trusting the water nymph's strong hand. He awoke, and slept, and awoke again.

He was by himself in a gentle pool. Deep enough that he

couldn't see the surface, shallow enough that sunlight reached to illuminate green water, green seaweed, and green rocks. One big rock was flat like a table and covered with knickknacks: pebbles, coins, a rusty dagger. An old jar stuffed with black feathers. A human skull? Dan shivered despite the warm water; Nellie was the strangest and most dangerous friend he had.

This must be the same pool where Nellie took him when he sought her help against Maggitch. Dan shivered again. That had been his first big gamble in Inland: Maggitch had truenamed Maggie, and Dan had beseeched help from cannibal Nellie. For some reason she had saved him and Maggie instead of eating them, and he didn't think her fight against Maggitch had been easy. He looked more closely at the skull. Good, it was way too big to be a child, and those feathers—Maggitch had started the fight in huge magpie form.

Dan drifted around the pool. The green rocks were embedded in golden sand. Here and there were some kind of shellfish, mussels or clams or something. A few minnows darted past. Where was Nellie?

Dan went to sleep hungry when the greens faded to black. All remained black when he awoke, alert. Some disturbance in the water? Yes, something swished and burbled. "Nellie?" called Dan. But it didn't feel like Nellie, and Dan backed into an alcove. When light finally returned there was nothing to see but Nellie's pool.

It felt like midday when Nellie returned and said, "Nellie remembers Dan bringing Outland food. Now Nellie brings Dan Inland food." She handed him a trout, gutted but raw.

"Nellie, did you return in the middle of the night and leave again?"

"Nellie fished. Nellie searched," she replied.

"Searched for what?"

"For the day Nellie seeks. Eat!"

Dan looked at his trout. "Thank you, Nellie. You even cleaned it. But I can't eat raw fish."

"Does Dan want to leave Nellie, cook on shore?"

Dan pondered for a moment. Nellie's pool was very peaceful. "No. It's nice here. But I am hungry."

"Then Dan will change," pronounced Nellie, taking the fish from him.

"Change how?"

But Nellie only chewed the trout, watching Dan over it with wide eyes.

It was hard to keep track of the passing days, but at some point Dan found himself eating raw trout with gusto. He had a pang of worry that he was turning into Gollum, but he didn't feel like saying "precious," and he wasn't growing webs between fingers or toes. But then he couldn't remember if Gollum's digits were webbed anyway.

"Nellie," asked Dan, "What's going on?"

"Nellie searches for the day. Nellie has almost found it."

"The day for what?"

"The Long Swim. Will Dan Outlander take the Long Swim with Nellie?"

"That was already a pretty long swim just to get me here from where you found me."

Nellie hissed. "Dan Outlander has a stiff mind. Nellie speaks of the Long Swim."

"OK, you mentioned that to me a long time ago. What is the Long Swim?"

Nellie replied, "The eternal swim."

Suddenly Dan felt very sad. "Nellie, will you be coming back?"

But Nellie would not explain any further, only repeating that Dan had a stiff mind.

The next morning, Dan said, "Nellie, I don't really understand, but it sounds like you are going away. I don't want to say goodbye to you, but I can't go on the Long Swim even if I want to. I have to leave Inland forever unless I marry Maggie before the next full moon."

Nellie scowled. "Fairy rules for fairies. Nellie rules for Nellie. Dan swims with Nellie as many moons as he wants."

Could this be true? Dan could stay in Inland, but with Nellie instead of Maggie? He licked fish from his fingers and tongued free a bit that had lodged between his teeth. He knew the stories about lotus-eaters forgetting their quests, and maybe that was part of what was happening to him, but it wasn't completely that. Nellie was Inland as much as Maggie—more really—and he loved being part of Inland. And this pool wasn't like the pavilion in the Blossomtree clearing. This was both stronger and gentler. It gave the choice of staying or going, but said why would you ever choose to leave such peace and loveliness? Go if you want, but you know that anywhere you go after this will be plain and dry.

And whatever the Long Swim was, it sounded mysterious and exciting. But then a thought crept into Dan's brain. Was it death? Was the Long Swim death? Nellie would never tell him, even if she knew. And Dan remembered the moon. He needed to see the moon, but he couldn't surface from the magical depths by himself.

"Nellie, please take me to the top tonight? A little after midnight."

It was thrilling to swim holding Nellie's hand, because it made him practically a water creature himself. He jackknifed beside her like a porpoise or seal, and in the joy of it they circled and dove, then finally surfaced so fast that they shot completely out of the water and fell back laughing.

And there shone the moon, not far above the eastern horizon, waxing gibbous. Dan figured he had three more days.

Dan heard a quiet splash and looked at the shore behind him. The blue stag and white doe were drinking cautiously, by turns keeping watch while the other muzzled the water. They shone in the moonlight. Weird to see them so often when they had been so scarce in the past.

On the other shore was a campfire and a seated figure.

"Let's go back down, Nellie," said Dan. He started to dive but she pulled him back.

"Not yet, Dan Outlander. Dan must visit shore. The Long Swim must be chosen with knowing heart. Nellie awaits Dan's choice here. Remember that Dan must stay in water; if Dan chooses the dry he must first kiss Nellie or die."

Dan sighed and nodded and swam toward the fire. He swam as slowly as he could, and when he got close enough that he thought he recognized the figure he stopped and treaded water. But the man by the fire had seen him and was beckoning. Finally Dan swam on until the water was shallow enough for him to stand. The man hailed him.

It was Billy. Billy who had invited him to Inland and always seemed to help him. But the same Billy had sent him on quests where he many times faced death, and ended with him about to be sent home with nothing.

"What do you want, Billy Portman?"

"Gatemoodle needs you, Dan. Inland needs you."

"Or is it Billy Gates? Or Johnny Quickfoot?"

"I have gone through the ages by many names, as you know." Billy gestured at the gibbous moon. "But time grows short, and my names are not important."

"But names are important, aren't they? My whole time here has been about my truename, and Maggie's, and Sister's. And now I have a new truename that I don't know. And funnily enough, I can't feel who I am anymore. I was the bored kid with a crush on the Goth girl. Then I was the guy who sought First Changing Beast in Inland and loved a beautiful fairy. Then I was the guy who was engaged to the fairy princess and whose truename changed when he defeated Sister. But you're not going to let me marry Maggie, are you—you, and First Changing Beast, and this whole stupid world? So finally I'm the loser who gets sent back home?"

Billy bowed his head. "It is very hard. 'Finally'—perhaps that is too long a word, yet hard it is. None of us understand the choices of First Changing Beast; not I, not Crackerbones, not Mother Ferny. Nor the King or Queen of the Fairies, nor Fir Darrig. But Inland needs you."

"I think I've done about enough for Inland. I found First Changing Beast. I neutralized Sister. Time for Inland to do something for me, not kick me out. And you, you've sponsored this whole stupid thing, time for you to do something for me!"

"Dan, what did I say when we first met, many moons ago in your Outland house, about what visitors from your land found in mine?"

"That we found beauty and riches and love." All these words were burned in Dan's brain.

"There was more," said Billy.

Dan gritted his teeth. "And mortal danger. And if we returned we were never unchanged."

Billy shrugged.

"Yeah, OK, that's all happened, and so you didn't promise anything else." Dan was shouting now. This was the maddest he'd been at Billy since the Gatekeepers had first given him their vague unhinged quest to find FCB—and now Maggie wasn't here to calm him down. "Well I didn't promise anything either! Anyway, there's nothing I could do to help even if I wanted to. Can't marry Maggie, or did you forget that?"

"I deem if you talk to your friends you will know what you can do. It will still be yours to choose, yea or nay. But come talk to your friends."

"Nellie knows a way I can stay."

"The Long Swim?" Billy sighed. "Only the water people understand it. But I will be sad if you take the Long Swim, for I fear then we will never meet again. Your friends will be sad."

"Stop guilting me!"

Dan turned and swam, fast this time, to where Nellie waited. She asked, "Nellie's kiss? Or Nellie's swim?"

"Take me to your pool and tell me about the Long Swim." Nellie flashed her sharp teeth in a smile and took Dan's hand.

They conversed long that night, but in watery words expressing liquid thoughts. It was the gleam of fishes, the wisdom of octopi, the flight of fountains. It was typhoon power and seahorse shyness. It was the clever coordination of shoals of herring evading seals, and it was the crunch of seal jaws on herring flesh. It was mats of plankton glowing on the surface and predatory anglerfish glowing in bottomless depths. It was trout song, whale song, gull song, the song of wind and wave on beaches sandy or crunchy with rocks and shells. But always it was like when Dan had a dream and knew he was dreaming and watched it all slip away even as he first grasped it.

And in the morning Dan said, "I am sorry, Nellie. I cannot go with you."

"Nellie knows. Dan knows Nellie. Dan knows Maggie. Only Nellie thinks Dan does not know Dan. But Nellie will take Dan to Gatemoodle."

They grasped hands. Dan wished it would take a very long time, but Nellie's pool was close to Gatemoodle and it felt like they arrived as soon as they started. At the very spot where Dan had brought Nellie back to life after Noggles killed her they stood, both with one foot on shore and one in the water. The very spot where Dan brought her back to life by using the Makeless Made spell, and brought upon himself the curse that he must leave Inland forever in three full moons.

Dan hugged Nellie and whispered, "I would do it again."

Nellie kissed him and whispered back, "Nellie met Dan a gleaming day, now both they go on their own way, Nellie below and Dan above, will Dan remember Nellie's love?"

# EZ DAKIA BERE BENEUTAKO
# IZENA

 *N*ellie's weird cousins keened softly. The ripples widened where she dove. As they brushed the shore at Dan's feet the air pulsed in rhythmic accord. Dan watched the water grow still and flat, and only as he turned toward Gatemoodle did he realize the pulsing continued. As though the air swayed from normal to thick to normal to heavy. He checked his own pulse in case that's what he was really noticing, but the rhythm was different. This wasn't like the pulsing just before First Changing Beast married itself, this was horrible. Dan was seized with anxiety that something unbearable would happen if his pulse synced with what was around him. He hugged his poncho to his chest and strode toward the Hall.

And stopped. It took him a moment to figure out what was wrong. He saw the old Hall on the hill, its solid wooden door closed, but that was normal. He couldn't hear any voices from the wedding venue in the valley beyond, but probably everybody had gone home while he was away.

It was the colors. The tree trunks were brown, leaves and grass were green, the scattered flowers were red and yellow and blue. But it was the browns and greens and reds and yellows and blues of Outland. Pretty, but not the elvish extra they should be. Only the venerable beams and logs of the Hall itself shone the way they should.

It frightened Dan, so instead of going straight up to the Hall he turned left and slipped into the trees that lined the approach road. The pulsing didn't get louder, but that was almost worse: it beat tediously on and on.

Footsteps on the road. Dan crouched and looked through the branches. Josh! Dan stepped out.

Josh jumped. "There you are! Where the hell have you been? Are you all right? One second it's happy happy time with you and Maggie finally getting married, and then you get grabbed by Little Shop of Horror plants and whisked off. We worried you were dead!"

"I'm not dead, but I'm not exactly all right. Inland, or FCB, or something doesn't want us to get married. But are you OK? Did awful things happen here too? What's been going on?"

"A lot. Come on up to the hall and we'll tell you. Alice and Graci and Maggie are there, even the Green Goblin too, we've been taking turns walking around hoping to find you. Hey, that's a real crappy poncho you got there."

They started up the hill, and Dan said, "Even though they don't want me to get married, I've been allowed back here somehow, so we're going to make it happen. I need to marry Maggie and soon, Josh, I've only got two days left. I suppose all the wedding guests are long gone, but I don't see why Billy or Ferny can't do the honors."

"As far as everyone being gone, well it's complicated. Look." Josh gestured down to the valley as it came in sight.

All the benches were still occupied, but the guests were unmoving. Not slumped over like sleeping or dead, just stiff. First Changing Beast alone was not in that strange state, but even he was nearly motionless, standing on the dais in Lion Man form, arms crossed, gazing at the audience.

"What in the world?" said Dan.

"Come on." Josh pushed open the door and they stepped inside.

It felt right. The old wooden structure exuded its usual friendly welcome that grew from the spells of amity that bound it. Better yet, the pulsing stopped as soon as Josh shut the massive door. But the Gatekeepers huddled on stools in front of the stove, holding hands in a circle, heads bowed. Only Billy glanced up and gave Dan a brief nod.

"Found him!" shouted Josh.

Maggie, Alice, and Graciela sprang up from the table in back, followed by the Green Goblin. In seconds Maggie was in Dan's arms. It felt too good to let go.

But it wasn't long before Josh was shouting, "OK, OK, break it up! Two words, Dan: Two days!"

Dan let go but kept gazing into Maggie's eyes. "Let's get Billy or Mother Ferny to marry us. We can stay in the safe hall where those stupid plants can't grab me again."

"Oh, I wish it were so!" said Maggie. "But look at Billy! Look at the others! They have no thoughts or words to spare from their task of holding Gatemoodle together."

"What are you talking about? What's happening to this place?"

"We think it is the failure of the weddings," said Alice.

"Well, they're the ones who made our wedding fail! So why is Inland falling apart or going gray if Inland chose to stop the wedding?"

"Oh, it stopped our wedding but wants another!" cried Maggie.

"Let me tell it," said Graciela. "After you disappeared, Maggie was still up there in front of FCB, and the grass held her feet. Those vines grabbed the Green Goblin. You really OK me calling you that?"

"Sure," answered the Goblin. "And I'm already married, and gay, and that should have been enough to make it obvious we weren't a match. But what Graciela hasn't mentioned yet is that the world kept getting duller, and the celebrants more still. By the time I said No they could hardly move. Man, it was grim. So I gave them a couple lines of a poem I thought they needed." And the Goblin began to chant:

'Try to praise the mutilated world.
Remember June's long days,
and wild strawberries, drops of rosé wine.
The nettles that methodically overgrow
the abandoned homesteads of exiles.
You must praise the mutilated world.

"There's more, but I stopped because it didn't seem to be helping."

"I was watching First Changing Beast," said Maggie. "It understood you, I could see that in its face. But it is true that the world grew grayer and the people more still."

"'Then it was Josh's turn," resumed Graciela.

"Josh was supposed to marry Maggie?" Dan gaped.

"I'm only beginning. Well Josh just started laughing, and Maggie kissed him on the cheek and turned away, and the plants released him but not Maggie. Alice was next."

"Inland turns out to be gender fluid," Alice put in. "But I am pissed off. All along I've wondered why FCB chose Josh and me to come back with you this time by giving his statues to us."

"I'm glad you've been here, as friends and help both," said Dan.

"Well, maybe we helped," said Alice, "but I don't think that's why we were chosen. Sneaky FCB was planning all along on using us as mortals who could marry Maggie."

"Alice and Maggie just smiled at each other and hugged and turned away," resumed Graciela. "The plants released Alice, and it was my turn. Pretty much the same thing happened."

"I still don't understand the Goblin's poem," said Josh. "But that's me, and that's the Goblin, and it doesn't matter right now. What matters is they're probably going to attempt another marriage. There's one more mortal-born to try."

"Wait a minute," said Dan. "This doesn't make any sense. We're in Inland, and in the fairy tales the mortals in fairyland don't have that kind of power, like to refuse a wedding they insist on, I mean."

"Surely it is because the needful time for the wedding is almost upon us," said Maggie. "Inland already weakens, lacking the six thousand moon ceremony. And they are terrified as they taste a barren future. I am terrified. If Inland becomes Outland, where will I be?"

"Then let's try again. They have to accept us after all the other pairings failed." Dan grabbed Maggie's hand and ran for the door, glancing at the sad Gatekeepers as he passed. His friends followed, but Dan and Maggie sprinted ahead with his Inland strength and her fairy speed. Out the door, not slowed by the pulsing air, down the hillside, to the beginning of the aisle with its now dull flowers. And there they lurched to a stop, grasped ankle and knee by writhing vines.

They would have lurched to a stop under their own power. Josh muttered "Oh my God." Dr. Green—Greenjack—the Prince—was already standing before First Changing Beast. Dan clutched Maggie to him and saw tears running down her face. Now Inland was replacing Maggie with a different fairy for the wedding? For the first time it struck Dan that it really, truly might not work out. In all the books sadness was described as gray, or black, but that wasn't right. Sadness was like a cool, clear light.

The Prince spoke, and Dan began to hope again. "First Changing Beast, although she does not yet stand beside me, I know whom you intend me to wed. And I know that a wedding between mortal and fay is needful to save Inland. But the only partners who could seal such a wedding with love are Dan and Maggie. Maggie you tried to pair with others, so it is only Dan whom you refuse. You have not told us why. That is no surprise, since none of us here remember you using speech. Yet in my role in Outland where I was banished I championed open speech, and this I deem to be one Outland trait that we have more need of here. I cannot compel you, and I would not compel you if I could, but to help all of us find a solution that helps us all, and Inland, and you, I beseech you: why cannot Dan marry Maggie?"

The pulsing slowed, but just as Dan let himself feel relieved, it grew louder. Slow, but louder and louder until even with his hands over his ears his head hurt. Branches cracked and the ground shook.

Then came utter stillness. And in the stillness came the lion's roar that was also a man's quiet, firm speech:

"Ez dakia bere beneutako izena."

Dr. Green nodded. "I see. He does not know his truename, so it cannot be known if his purpose and place are with Maggie."

So there it was. His changed truename, the very thing that had protected him from Mrs. Westerley, was blocking him from Maggie. Dan wanted to yell that he was certain his purpose and place were with Maggie, but he knew that would be tossed aside as mortal ignorance. He yelled anyway, but his voice was muffled as though the air around him were thick cotton.

Dr. Green continued. "But First Changing Beast, this will not do. I know the partner you intend for me. As much as I detest her past actions, I would sacrifice myself and wed her to prevent the fading of Inland—if she were my only concern. But I will not do this to my patient in Outland. I will not do this to my friend in Inland. I will not do this to the man who freed me by freeing you. I will not do this to Dan. Instead I will help Dan learn his truename. Let Dan and Maggie wed." He kicked aside the plants that gripped him, strode from the dais, and took a seat beside his parents. The poor King and Queen! After such a brief loving reunion, flesh was again peeling from their skulls. Dan peered more closely at Dr. Green and saw it was happening to him too.

It was Sister who was wanted for the bride, of course, and at dusk they found her, and Mrs. Westerley too, although Dan never learned where they had been hiding. A fairy whom Dan recognized as one of the uncaring guards who had taken them from Sister's tower to prison in the fairy city had been appointed the groom. "That fairy is no one special at all," said Maggie. "I think they do not care what mortal and fairy wed, as long as it is not us." She and Dan gripped hands tightly; it looked like their last chance was about to disappear.

Sister paced slowly to the dais. The fairy held out his hand to her. Dan held his breath and felt time stop. And then Sister slapped the hand away. "Ha! Still Sister!" whispered Josh.

And Sister cried out, "I will not marry this one! I will not marry any other! It is true my curse has been lifted, but that does not make everything sunshine and sparkles."

"The curse can't be lifted because I don't love her," whispered Dan.

Josh elbowed him. "Shut up! I'm going to do that every time you try to talk them out of it."

The Green Goblin said, "There's many kinds of love, bro."

Sister was still talking. "I feel freedom that I never thought to feel in this life of nails and ice. I no longer desire lordship over this world. But neither do I desire to save it. Some hurts run too deep." She was shaking her fist at the Fairy King. "We are not in some Outland fairy tale that ends happily ever after. We are in grim reality, and I am no Sugar Plum to sweeten it for you. I spit on you for giving ice and nails to my sister and the one she adores. Let the lovers marry, I will not take their place." She stomped from the dais.

Dan hugged Maggie and said, "We're the only option left!" as Josh said, "Yay, Sister!"

But the vines tightened around Dan's ankles, and the moon rose, one day from the Full.

"Let us go inside." It was Fir Darrig. "The plants allow you that direction."

The horrible pulsing had resumed, and it was a relief to enter the Hall and escape it. Good old Gatemoodle had been there from the beginning. But how much longer?

"I can hold Billy's place in the circle, though only a short time for I be not a Gatekeeper," said the strange red dwarf. "Billy wants talk with you."

"But first, Mr. Darrig, where is Turtle?" asked Maggie.

Fir Darrig smiled. "We thank you for your concern. Turtle munches hay, safe in Gatemoodle stables. The circle is strong—for now." He took Billy's place between Mother Ferny and Crackerbones.

Instead of coming straight to them Billy drank a pitcher of water and munched a shriveled apple.

"Outland food?" asked Dan.

Billy nodded. "One of our last, and much needed. But even so strengthened, sooner or later we will fail, and Gatemoodle will also go gray. Let us sit and talk."

Even before they dropped into comfortable chairs, Dan asked, "Billy, there's no way First Changing Beast will change his mind about my truename, is there?"

"Nay. Though really it is not First Changing Beast deciding. The Beast speaks for Inland. And strange though it may sound, that is better for you."

That made no sense and Dan ignored it. "And there's also no way I can figure out my truename in twenty-four hours. I don't have a clue."

Billy nodded.

"And maybe part of me finding my truename is in Outland, but I know—we all know—that part of it has to be here too, here in Inland. I mean, I belong here as much as there. So I'm never going to find it, which I guess doesn't matter because who cares about truenames in Outland?"

"The Prince told me they matter very much there," said Billy. "But—"

Dan rolled his eyes and snorted, "Psychology."

"I agree psychology is dumb," said Josh, "but c'mon, Green always steered you right."

"This is such a sad time that it's hard to think, but your truename is probably a metaphor in our world," said Graciela.

"OK, great, some important metaphor, but I still can't find it in time to marry Maggie."

"First Changing—" began Billy.

Dan interrupted, "And so I'll never find it because I can never come back." He looked at Maggie. "And I'm not just being selfish. Inland is starting to go as bad as Sister wanted to make it. I'm kind of with her, I'm not sure Inland deserves saving. It's kind of treating me like crap, after all I've done for it. But I care about you, Billy, and Mother Ferny and even Crackerbones who always wanted to eat me. And most of all I care for Maggie. What's going to become of all of you with no wedding? What will become of Maggie?"

Alice interrupted. "Excuse little me for speaking up, but isn't everybody forgetting something? Dan has Breaklock, right? Permanent ability to go back and forth? So doesn't that cancel the Makeless Made business about never coming back?"

Dan looked at Graciela and shook his head, but before he said anything Billy also shook his head and said, "Makeless Made is more powerful even than Breaklock. But—"

"So that's out too," said Dan.

"Dan, Billy has been trying to tell us—you—something about First Changing Beast and Inland," said Maggie.

"I don't care about First Changing Beast and Inland! I care about you, and our friends here, and mostly you."

"Remember what I told you beside Nellie's pool?" asked Billy.

"Nellie Longarms? You were with that weirdo?" asked Josh.

Dan waved him off. "Too much to catch up on, too little time," he said. "Yes, Billy, you said I would figure out what to do, and that didn't make sense then and doesn't make sense now."

"I said talk to your friends here and you would figure out what to do. And now I leave you to that. I must relieve Fir

Darrig. He will tell you what I meant about First Changing Beast and Inland. Also, he has something for you."

Billy left, and soon Fir Darrig sat where Billy had been seated and began to talk. "Hard it is to explain Inland matters to Outland minds. It is good that First Changing Beast did not make the rule. First Changing Beast is one mind, or two, or perhaps a little more. But Inland is multitudinous. You were with the water lady, and she offered you a way to escape Makeless Made, a watery way, am I right? And you did not take it."

"I did not."

"I offer you a jewel way. I do not understand it fully myself. Breaklock has power to pass gates in part because it is of Outland and Inland both. I have a jewel that is of Outland and Inland both. It will not pass gates on its own but can mesh with Breaklock."

Dan imagined some gorgeous gem, but Fir Darrig reached for his clattering necklace and unclipped Dan's iPhone. "You gifted me this Outland jewel. It has taken in Inland as I wore it. I gift it back to you."

"I thank you," said Dan. This was definitely weird, but exciting weird. Sounded like he could get back to Inland after all! If he could figure out how to save it by talking to his friends. Of course no phones worked in Inland. The screen glimmered and cycled through incredible colors that Apple had never installed, but the clock that was visible was stuck at 7:00. Which felt good, the basic magic number!

Fir Darrig said, "The number is the years that must pass between visits."

Oh.

"Now I leave you to your friends," said the dwarf.

* * *

"SO NOW IT's just us—I was going to say 'normal humans,' but I guess you don't completely qualify, Maggie," said Josh. "Sorry, that was rude."

Maggie smiled. "I am too sad to tease, but do not worry, Josh."

The Green Goblin said, "You never really considered me normal either, did you?"

"Well, maybe I've grown up a little here too," answered Josh.

"I don't think any of us are exactly normal," said Graciela.

"But guys," said Alice, "we're supposed to help Dan figure out what to do. Dan, tell us what happened after those plants grabbed you, let's start there."

"Well, they dropped me at the Mad Prince's Castle." Dan furrowed his brows and peered at the Green Goblin. "Do you remember it?"

"Of course not, first time here, remember?"

"Well, you weren't there this time but you sort of were before."

"Stop that, Dan!" interjected Josh. "Confusing us with crazy Inland won't help."

Maggie smiled again. "Then again it might. It was a mutilated phantasm of you, Goblin. Oh we had such fun, even when it was frightening. I wish it could go on forever."

"We're working on that, Maggie," said Alice. "Go on, Dan."

That word "mutilated" piqued something in Dan's brain but he couldn't pull it out. He continued telling his friends about his journey: the not-so-friendly dwarf miners, the mountain ridge that he and Maggie had climbed a different time, the three weird floating heads ("Oh my God," whispered Josh), the woods where he worried about wolves.

"Then came the Question Gnome. I hate this guy. He was there the other time too, and I call him that because all he does is respond to questions with stupid inscrutable questions of his own. This time he asked me, 'Is what the goblin says true?' Oh that's it!"

"You know what to do?" asked Graciela.

"No, it's the goblin. I thought Question Gnome meant Crackerbones or Loosejaw, you know, an Inland goblin, but Crackerbones is in the silent circle and Loosejaw is in the frozen audience. He meant you, Green Goblin, you and your poem. Inland's all messed up. My life and Maggie's here are all messed up. So he was asking if it's true that I have to praise the mutilated world."

He and Maggie held each other's eyes. Praise a world without each other?

The Goblin watched them, and then shrugged. "I try to praise it. The whole supervillain thing was my life, remember?"

Dan remembered. Back in school the Goblin had been a Goth kid that Dan avoided as a stupid loser.

"The strawberries and nettles both," said Maggie under her breath.

"What happened next?" asked Alice.

"Next was Nellie Longarms, and then Billy." Dan used to worry that Maggie would be jealous of his feelings for Nellie, but he sensed that they were both beyond jealousy now. He described her temptation of the Long Swim that would keep him in Inland, Billy's plea that he return to Gatemoodle, and his watery realization that he did not want Inland without Maggie or any of his friends. "I guess my truename doesn't lie in that direction."

Maggie snuggled against him. "So it was kind of a memory trip," she said. "All those old friends. I even like hearing about the land again, and the big trees and the wolves who were not there."

"Yeah, and I forgot to mention, the big blue deer was there. Helpful again, he led me to Nellie."

"He has always been helpful," said Maggie. "The first time was in those same woods, he led us to the silvan glade." She nudged Dan and they smiled a private smile.

"What's the story again about why a deer is being so helpful?" asked Alice.

"Because he is my Outland father," replied Maggie. "Oh, it is too complicated to describe."

Dan felt the same way. He still didn't know what he was supposed to do, but he was done talking. He held Maggie closer.

"I'll tell it," said Graciela. "We learned the story from the Fairy Queen. It involves my Tia Josefina too. She and Maggie's Outland father were lovers after he divorced Mrs. Westerley. ("Which we don't blame him for at all," interrupted Josh.)

"They went to Inland Mexico, just exploring, not knowing anything about Sister or abuse and the Old Ways. But the Fairy Queen found them because she thought that with her help, Maggie's Outland father could limit the King's cruelty. She charmed Maggie's Outland father such that if anyone loved his two daughters, they would be free. You know, he's Sister's biological father, so she figured he had a better chance than anyone of loving Sister. Then all he had to do was love Maggie, and Maggie's easy to love." Graciela gave Maggie a quick hug. "Anyway, the King didn't want Maggie's Outland father to be able to free the girls, or tell anyone else how to do it, so he turned him into a blue deer. There's more about my aunt, but it makes me sad, and there's too much sadness here already.

"Anyway, that's where the thing about someone needing to love both Sister and Maggie comes from. And Dan, like it or not, the Goblin here is right that there are different kinds of love, and you showed Sister one kind when you not only didn't kill her but found a way to release her from truenaming agony. But to answer your question, Alice, that's why a deer is so helpful—he's Maggie's adoptive father!"

Suddenly Dan knew what he needed to do for Inland. And the cool, clear light of sadness saturated everything.

"Oh, but one more thing," continued Graciela. "Dan has a kind of horn that can summon the blue deer. He used it during the Battle of Gatemoodle, and that deer came and just mowed down the malkins. Do you still have that horn, Dan?"

"Yeah, of course. I wouldn't lose something with that power; it's always in my pack. You know, the white doe was there on my journey too. And remember, they both helped us through the Chattertree Woods." He stretched. "We've talked long enough, and we better get some sleep. Tomorrow will be a big day—starting with a wedding."

The others chorused variations of "Wait, what?" and "You've figured it out?" Without replying, Dan took Maggie's hand and they stepped outside and gazed at the sky. The awful pulsing was still going on, but Dan knew he would stop it tomorrow. A glorious moon shone straight overhead. Dan could see the tiny dark sliver on its side that would be filled in to complete the orb when the next night came.

# WEDDING DAY

*I*t ended up being simple, really. The next morning Dan and his friends stood with the Gatekeepers in front of the Hall. As soon as the Gatekeepers had broken the circle, the Hall sighed and looked sad, but Dan had assured them that it wouldn't be for long, and they trusted him.

First Changing Beast stood motionless on the dais, gazing at all the wedding guests petrified on their benches. The air pulsed as though massive artillery approached.

Dan took the horn from his pocket and blew upon it an impossible note, sweet like a wood thrush greeting the dawn, loud like a waterfall filled with spring snowmelt; gentle as the tread of a fawn on fresh grasses yet clashing like antler against antler as bucks battled for dominance.

From the wooded hillside came an answering bugle.

The pulsing stopped.

The great blue stag walked into the wedding valley, the white doe at his side. They stood before First Changing Beast, in front of the guests who all came to life. And the mortal man turned blue stag wedded the white fairy doe.

And Maggie hugged the stag that was her Outland father, and he nuzzled her face. And then the stag and the doe sprang away to their woodland life.

And the guests burst into song, song so rich and beautiful that Dan wondered if the whole land was singing. Flowers never before seen burst from bough and loam. Browns, greens, reds, yellows, blues, and colors Dan had no name for flared together in sublime dance.

Dan looked at the dais. First Changing Beast was gone. Dan had hoped to say farewell to it, but somehow this seemed more fitting.

He turned to his friends. "Guys, Maggie and I are going for a walk today. I'll be back before moonrise, and I'll take you home. The last use of Breaklock."

"And you can land us when we left, right?" asked Josh.

Josh was grimacing, and Dan knew he wanted to say more but there was nothing more to say. Alice was sniffling. Even Graciela had pushed her glasses aside to rub her eyes. "I'll land you when you left." That would be a little tricky; Josh and Alice had come with him this time, Graciela was already here from an earlier trip, and the Green Goblin got here just a few days ago. But Dan and Breaklock were old companions by now; they could make it happen. And Graciela had to be last.

And now for goodbyes. Dan turned to his former therapist first. "Hey, Dr. Green. That's what I want to call you, in memory of when all this started. But maybe I'll see you in Outland? The Gates of Inland are open now, so you can go back and forth, right? Be Prince here but still a therapist there?"

"I must spend almost all my time here in Inland. My father leaves the throne now to dwell with my mother at the Knoll of the Other. He is tired, tired from the Old Ways, and they desire rest and rejuvenation and togetherness with their new-grown flesh and skin. So I will be Regent, with much in the Marrowland to set aright."

"Wow! Congratulations!"

"But I have my patients still to consider, so I will go first to Outland to close my practice and refer them to other therapists that I trust. Perhaps I will see you there?"

"Home won't be my first stop." Dan smiled with one side of his mouth. "'Home.' Not sure where home is anymore. Anyway, I may not be back there for a while. So just in case: thanks for everything. You did so much for us here—like killing the hoga and finding Moonmallow for Maggie. But I think I'm most grateful for when you were my therapist. You steadied me when Inland and Maggie were making me crazy. So, well, thanks."

Dan choked a little and started to turn away, but Dr. Green spoke up. "Since we may not see each other, let me leave you this to consider: Not knowing your truename both saved you from Sister and blocked you from marrying Maggie. Bitter irony to be sure. But is it also something more?"

"Like what?" asked Dan, and then laughed. "Oh great, we're out of time." He stuck out his hand for a handshake that turned into a quick hug.

Then Dan stood in front of Crackerbones. Seriously ugly Crackerbones with his pale green mottled skin, his lank hair, his sharp teeth. Dan remembered how scared he and Maggie had been when they first encountered him, before they knew he was a Gatekeeper or even knew what a Gatekeeper was. And he remembered how much Crackerbones scared him from time to time threatening to eat him. But Crackerbones had also been a staunch ally of Gatemoodle and an aid to Dan when needed, even saving Dan and his friends from death by risking his own in the caverns of the South American mukis. They nodded to each other, and Dan extended his hand. He was a little worried there would be some special weird goblin handshake that he didn't know, but it turned out to be normal. They shook hands firmly and turned away.

Mother Ferny was next. She sniffed the air and said, "You cooked very tastily, Dan, but I sense you now begin to prepare another dish." Yeah, that was Mother Ferny. When he first came to Inland she thought he was too raw to succeed in finding First Changing Beast. Maybe he had been then, but definitely no longer. But she was probably right that he needed to cook in a different way now. "Goodbye, Mother Ferny," he said, and they hugged.

And now for Billy Portman, or Billy Gates, or whatever. Billy had pissed him off sometimes, but it was he that recruited Dan for Inland, and he had always personified Gatemoodle and security as Dan encountered insane dangers. "Goodbye, Billy. You were there from the beginning, and you've meant so much to me. And this seems silly, but one of the things that I will miss most about Inland is your cooking. And the way you always knew when I'd show up with my friends and have a meal ready. And your advice—really, just knowing you were here."

Billy responded, "No Outlander has ever deserved more thanks than you. My cooking and my advice would have been in vain if someone other than you had received them. And remember, Dan, by succeeding in your quest to find First Changing Beast you have stopped the Gates of Inland from closing to us. Outland has changed since the days when we hobs would live in your houses and keep things in order. Even with the gates open we aren't welcome in the same way. Mostly my trips will be brief gatherings of Outland food. But there may be a time that I can visit."

"That would be wonderful, Billy."

"And after all this I see you not only as a hero. I see you as a friend. I wish that now, when because of you things have grown calmer, we could settle around the old Gatemoodle stove and share tales about your journeys here and about old Inland. But you have something more important to do."

Dan felt like there must be more to say, but at the same time looking into Billy's grandfather face was better than words. They hugged quickly, and the Gatekeepers turned and walked back into their Hall.

* * *

DAN AND MAGGIE walked all that day. With one mind they headed for the Moss Maidens' woods. This was where they had re-met after Dan had realized that Maggie was a fairy and had sent her on to Inland, unsure if he would ever see her again.

They spoke little. At one point Dan said, "You understand why I won't be able to use Breaklock anymore, don't you?"

And Maggie replied, "I understand."

Later she said, "We both know that even with Breaklock every seven years would be unbearable."

And Dan answered, "That would be a broken life. I wish it were not so but sometimes wishes do not matter. Amid all our adventures together we did not fix the world the way we wanted."

Maggie said, "Instead our adventures fixed it for others. We must love our broken world."

As one they said, "And even apart we will be part of each other."

They paused where a beam of sunlight fell onto a stream burbling through a dell. Maggie said, "We spent a night together here." As they strolled on she said, "In all the nights and days to come I want no other lover ever, but you should marry, Dan. You should have children that you can teach about Inland."

Dan wasn't sure that his recipe would turn out that way, but he said, "I hope you do find someone to love, and have your own children that you can teach about Outland."

Later yet, Dan said, "I wonder what will happen to Sister?"

"I will seek her out," said Maggie. "I may be able to help her with her loneliness. She may be able to help me with mine."

But mostly they walked together in silence, breathing in the rich scents of piney woods and mushrooms and old logs. And then came the approach of evening, and they needed to return to Gatemoodle before moonrise.

They placed on each other's fingers the wedding rings they had received from the Moss Maidens. And then they embraced. They embraced for each other, and they embraced for Inland, they embraced for the Gatekeepers and Fir Darrig and Turtle, and for Josh and Alice and Graciela. They embraced for all the time they had had together. Dan embraced Maggie and Maggie embraced Dan, and still they embraced. But they could not embrace forever.

# AFTER

*R*ays of the setting sun illuminated the striped tails of a pair of those big silent birds. Trogons, Dan remembered. The jungle cacophony was quieting down. The last tourists were leaving.

Dan sat beside Graciela on top of Palenque's biggest pyramid. It was cool that her father was honored by the caretakers here; they got to stay after hours.

"You're sure about this, Dan?"

Dan nodded. "It was always clear when your father made this for me that Pacal's bracelet and Yaxche's finger were only on loan." Señor Guillermo had made for Dan an amulet for entering Inland, in the form of a ringtoss toy, out of a stick from a gigantic ceiba tree and the bracelet of the longest ruling Lord of Palenque. It wasn't Breaklock yet with its limitless uses; that had required the nursing of the Moss Maidens and Mother Ferny. But it was a great trust that Dan meant to honor.

"When Father made that, you and I had barely met," said Graciela. "I assumed you were a jerk, un Americano típico. But you've been through so much, we've been through so much, and you are anything but a jerk. And I know what you'll be giving up. Maybe Pacal wouldn't mind you holding on to that."

"I think he would. And I think your father would. And anyway, I would. Your father made the amulet to help me get back to Maggie and find First Changing Beast, and those things I have done. I don't want to begin the search for my truename with a broken promise."

"That's your next quest, huh? Where will you begin?"

"I haven't seen Mom or Dad or my brother in ages. I'll start there."

"Makes sense." Graciela spread her arms to the ruins and the jungle beyond. "I bet there's a lot to find here too, and in New York."

"Oh, I'll be in touch. And I'll be checking messages." Dan pulled Fir Darrig's phone from his pocket and they laughed as they watched the strange colors undulating around the number seven. "I'll get a regular phone and text you the number."

Dan stood. He broke the cord holding bracelet and stick together and made it into a loop to hang his rings around his neck and under his shirt where they would not startle Outland eyes.

Then he handed the stick to Graciela. He climbed down the stairs that entered the center of the tomb where Pacal's casket had lain for centuries. Dan took a deep breath and placed the bracelet where it belonged.

# ACKNOWLEDGMENTS

A big Thank You to Joseph D'Agnese, who generously advised me on the production of *Wedding Day*. He writes lots of cool stuff; check it out!

And thanks to Donna, Joey, Susan, David, Sigmund, and Ronald.

ALSO BY JOHN ROSEGRANT

THE GATES OF INLAND

Book 1 Gatemoodle

Book 2 Kintravel

Book 3 Rattleman

Book 4 Marrowland

Book 5 Makeless Made

NONFICTION

Tolkien, Enchantment, and Loss: Steps on the Developmental Journey

www.ingramcontent.com/pod-product-compliance
Lightning Source LLC
Chambersburg PA
CBHW021242260626
47155CB00004BA/1276